THE MARIJUANA CHRONICLES

THE MARIJUANA CHRONICLES

EDITED BY **JONATHAN SANTLOFER**

This collection is comprised of works of fiction, with the exception of the nonfiction essays by Raymond Mungo and Rachel Shteir. In the fiction stories, all names, characters, places, and incidents are the product of the authors' imaginations. Any resemblance to real events or persons, living or dead, is entirely coincidental.

Published by Akashic Books

Hardcover ISBN-13: 978-1-61775-169-1
Paperback ISBN-13: 978-1-61775-163-9
Library of Congress Control Number: 2012954506

Illustrations by Jonathan Santlofer, except where noted

First printing

Akashic Books
PO Box 1456
New York, NY 10009
info@akashicbooks.com
www.akashicbooks.com

ALSO IN THE AKASHIC DRUG CHRONICLES SERIES:

The Cocaine Chronicles
edited by Gary Phillips & Jervey Tervalon

The Heroin Chronicles
edited by Jerry Stahl

The Speed Chronicles
edited by Joseph Mattson

Some of my finest hours have been spent on my back veranda, smoking hemp and observing as far as my eye can see.
—Thomas Jefferson

I now have absolute proof that smoking even one marijuana cigarette is equal in brain damage to being on Bikini Island during an H-bomb blast. —Ronald Reagan

I didn't inhale it, and never tried it again. —Bill Clinton

When I was a kid I inhaled frequently.
That was the point.
—Barack Obama

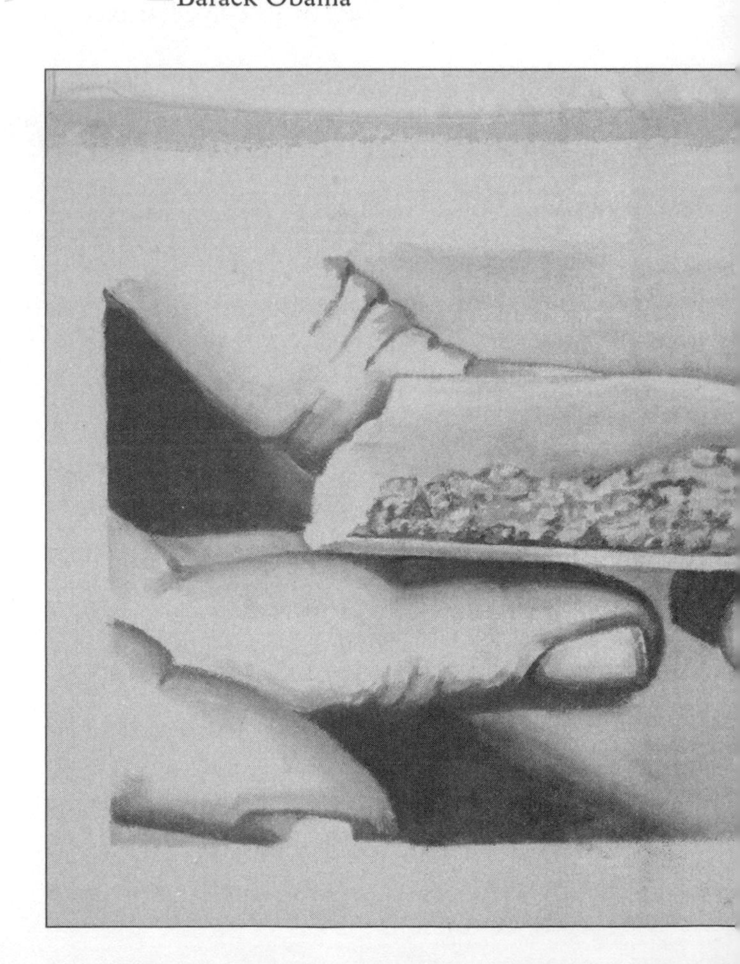

Forty million Americans smoked marijuana;
the only ones who didn't like it were Judge Ginsberg,
Clarence Thomas, and Bill Clinton. —Jay Leno

I think that marijuana should not only be legal,
I think it should be a cottage industry. —Stephen King

Researchers have discovered that chocolate
produces some of the same reactions in the brain as marijuana.
The researchers also discovered other similarities between the two
but can't remember what they are. —Matt Lauer

Hey, hey, hey, smoke weed every day. —Dave Chappelle

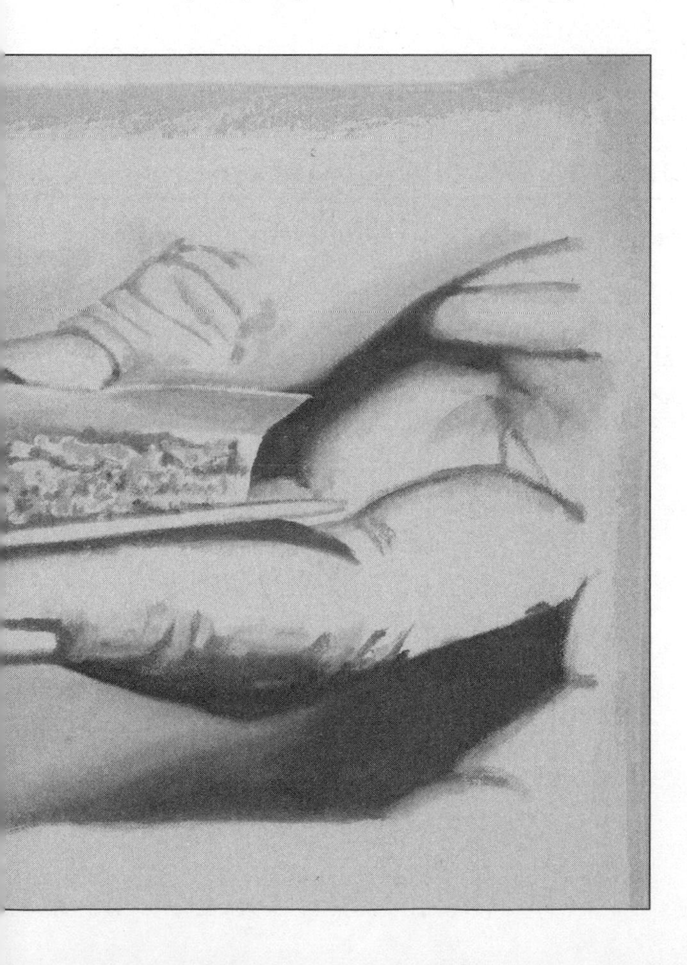

table of contents

PART III: RECREATION & EDUCATION

PART IV: GOOD & BAD MEDICINE

introduction
smoke: seventeen writers on going to pot
by jonathan santlofer

Pot. Grass. Hemp. Hash. Herb. Reefer. Ganja. Smoke. Spliff. Weed. Kush. Mary Jane. Cannabis. Tea. Blunt. Dope. Doobie.

Marijuana. The popular drug. The newsworthy drug. The everyman and everywoman drug. Medical marijuana. Recreational pot. A drug for the young, the old, and everyone in between. The drug that doesn't have you pawning the family silver along with your mother. The mellow—put on a Barry White CD, open a jug of vino, and send out for a dozen Dunkin' Donuts—drug. The cool drug. The no howling at the moon (well, maybe not) drug.

Whatever you want to call it, marijuana, cannabis, and hemp have been around for a long time. As a food in ancient China, a textile in 4000 BC Turkestan, referred to as "Sacred Grass" in Hindu texts long before Christ. Scythian tribes left cannabis seeds as offerings to the gods. Herodotus wrote on its recreational and ritualistic use. There is evidence that the Romans used it medicinally and the Jewish Talmud touted its euphoric properties. Syrian mystics introduced it to twelfth-century Egypt, and Arabs traded it along the coast of Mozambique. Marco Polo reported on hashish in his thirteenth-century journeys. Angolan slaves planted it between rows of cane on Brazilian plantations, the French and British grew cannabis and hemp in their colonies. George Washington cultivated it at Mount Vernon, and Thomas Jefferson grew it at Monticello. Around 1840 cannabis-based medicines became available in the US—*Le Club des Hashischins* (the Hashish-Eaters Club) was all the rage in Paris, and Turkish smoking parlors were opening in America. (All according to "A Short History of Cannabis," by Neil M. Montgomery, *Pot Night*, Channel 4 Television, March 4, 1995.)

As marijuana's popularity grew, the British taxed it, Napoleon banned it, Turkey made it illegal, Greece cracked down. In 1930, the US government ceded control of illegal drugs to the Treasury Department and Harry J. Anslinger, a prohibitionist zealot, was named the first commissioner of the Federal Bureau of Narcotics, a job he managed to hold until 1962. Anslinger waged war against marijuana with a nationwide campaign that linked pot smoking to insanity, and the *San Francisco Examiner* ran an editorial in 1923 supporting this belief:

> *Marihuana is a short cut to the insane asylum. Smoke marihuana cigarettes for a month and what was once your brain will be nothing but a storehouse of horrid specters.*

Clearly crazier and nastier than the vast majority of pot smokers would ever be, Anslinger went even further with his testimony at a Senate hearing, creating an abhorrent racial bias in regard to the drug:

> *There are 100,000 total marijuana smokers in the US, and most are Negroes, Hispanics, Filipinos, and entertainers. Their Satanic music, jazz and swing, result from marijuana usage. This marijuana causes white women to seek sexual relations with Negroes, entertainers, and any others.*

Though New York's mayor, Fiorello La Guardia, commissioned an in-depth study of the effects of smoking marijuana, which contradicted Anslinger's claims, it was condemned as unscientific and wholly disregarded by the crusading narcotics bureau chief.

Meanwhile, *Reefer Madness*, the full-length 1936 black-and-white propaganda movie, touted the dangers of a "new drug menace which is destroying the youth of America in alarmingly increasing numbers," that would ultimately cause "emotional disturbances . . . leading finally to acts of shocking violence . . . ending often in incurable insanity." Personally, I found the film's wild partying, sex, and even murder campy fun despite the pious preaching and bad acting. In the end, you just can't spell out the dangers of neon with neon and not make your audience want to try it!

The "culture of marijuana" was born (or reborn) sometime in the 1960s on college campuses across the US as students rallied against the Vietnam War and smoked pot publically. By 1965, it is believed, approximately one million Americans had tried the drug and within a few years that number had reached more than twenty million.

Nixon, Anslinger's heir apparent, tried to crush it with "Operation Intercept," an attempt to shut down border crossings between Mexico and the United States, while he raised the criminal stakes on marijuana possession so that a twenty-five-year-old Vietnam vet, Don Crowe, could be sentenced to fifty years in jail for selling less than an ounce. Though the National Commission on Marijuana and Drug Abuse released a 1972 study urging the decriminalization of smoking pot in the privacy of one's own home, Nixon disregarded it, created the DEA, gave it the authority to enter houses "without knocking," and began extensive wiretapping and intelligence-gathering on private citizens. The Reagan administration continued the war on drugs—who can forget first lady Nancy Reagan's famous "Just Say No" campaign?

With the leap from "just say no" to the astonishing decriminalization of recreational pot by Colorado and Washington in 2012, one can now say the actual *seeds* of change have been sown. Eighteen states plus Washington, DC have now legalized medical marijuana, and a host of medical literature points to evidence that the drug, in its myriad forms, can be used in the treatment of nausea and vomiting, anorexia and weight loss, spasticity, neurogenic pain, movement disorders, asthma, glaucoma, epilepsy, bipoloar disorder, and Tourette's syndrome. Recent studies with cannabis and cannabinoids show promise in treating arterial blockage, Alzheimer's disease, autoimmune diseases, and blood pressure disorders. The FDA acknowledges that "there has been considerable interest in its use for the treatment of a number of conditions, including glaucoma, AIDS wasting, neuropathic pain, treatment of spasticity associated with multiple sclerosis, and chemotherapy-induced nausea," but the agency has yet to approve it.

As Colorado governor John Hickenlooper points out, "Federal law still says marijuana is an illegal drug, so don't break out the Cheetos or Goldfish too quickly." While Colorado and Washington have made it legal to smoke, sell, or carry up to one ounce of marijuana, it will take some time to sort out the federal-versus-state issue. Despite the fact that there was no big funding in opposition to the legalization propositions—and despite a recent poll showing that "fifty percent of voters around the country now favor legalizing the drug for recreational use," cited by Benjamin Wallace-Wells in the December 3, 2012 issue of *New York*—the battle is hardly over.

With the marijuana debate, medical or otherwise, ongoing and persistent, I knew I wanted to echo that in this anthology with the inclusion of some writing about the facts. So *The Marijuana Chronicles* includes both fiction and nonfiction pieces. The writer and journalist Rachel Shteir supplied just that in a story about cannabis advocate and multiple sclerosis sufferer Julie Falco, whose brave fight for survival is at once human and legal. The issue raises its head again in former student radical Raymond Mungo's close-to-home tangled tale of the pursuit of legal and not-so-legal medical marijuana in California. The fact that the subject was taken up yet again but in an entirely fictional way in Thad Ziolkowski's short story about a medical marijuana farm felt not only like kismet but a reflection of the zeitgeist and confirmation that art and life always share a stage.

Hollywood has long reflected and embraced the change in attitude with such stoner star turns as Cheech and Chong's *Up in Smoke,* Sean Penn's hilarious Jeff Spicoli in *Fast Times at Ridgemont High,* Jane Fonda's pot-smoking hooker in *Klute,* Bridget Fonda in Quentin Tarantino's *Jackie Brown,* and the granddaddy of all counterculture stoner films, *Easy Rider,* wherein Peter Fonda (what is it with these Fondas?) introduces Jack Nicholson to his first smoke (and if you believe that was really Jack's first toke, you will believe anything). Diane Keaton needed a hit to relax her in *Annie Hall,* and Jeff Bridges played the ultimate stoner dude in *The Big Lebowski.*

Like film, literature has been no stranger to the drug, going back to Charles Baudelaire's 1860 *Artificial Paradises,* in which the French poet not only describes the effects of hashish but postulates it could be an aid in creating an ideal world. The pleasures, pains, and complexities of marijuana are more than hinted at in works by William S. Burroughs, Jack Kerouac, Allen Ginsberg, Henry Miller, Hunter S. Thompson, and Thomas Pynchon, to name just a few, and I hope this anthology will add to that legacy and keep the flame of pot literature burning bright.

National Book Award winner Joyce Carol Oates creates an instant classic for the genre in her dark tale of suburban-meets-urban weed consumption gone wrong, and Linda Yablonsky turns your head inside out with a pot-smoking, cross-dressing, gun-toting character as alluring as he is terrifying.

I never expected pothead zombies but that's just what Maggie Estep delivers in her zany and hilarious story. Cultural critic Edward M. Gómez gives us an urban tale at once real and idyllic, while Josh Gilbert takes us on a stoned journey through Hollywood hell. Amanda Stern offers us a coming-of-age cautionary tale with heart, soul, pot, *and* coke! And multi–award winning crime fiction author Lee Child could not help but write a story that will keep you guessing till the last line.

Marijuana crosses the ocean in Cheryl Lu-Lien Tan's story of pot-smoking friends in Singapore, and Abraham Rodriguez rocks us back to the future with his idiosyncratic blend of sci-fi and urban realism.

Bob Holman and Jan Heller Levi produce poems filled with poignancy and humor which remind us that poetry and pot have had a long acquaintance, while award-winning graphic artist Dean Haspiel creates a hallucinogenic world in pictures. As for me, I won't say how much of my story is real or imagined, but I do have a faded photo of my flower-painted face, which can be had for a price.

This diverse group of writers, poets, and artists makes it clear that there is no one point of view here. Each of them approaches the idea of marijuana with the sharp eye of an observer, anthropologist, and artist, and expands upon it. Some writing projects are difficult; this one was smooth and mellow and a continual pleasure.

As a survivor of the sex-and-drug revolution, I could never have imagined the decriminalization of my generation's forbidden fruit. Perhaps there is another Anslinger waiting in the wings, but practically every day a new article extols the virtues of medical marijuana and other states get ready to put the drug in the category of alcohol. Is it possible that in a few years it will be easier to buy a pack of joints than cigarettes? I don't know the answer to that but in the meantime I hope you will sit back, relax, and enjoy these wide-ranging tales of the most debated and discussed drug of our time. Though, according to former California governor Arnold Schwarzenegger, "That is not a drug, it's a leaf."

Jonathan Santlofer
New York City
April 2013

PART I

DANGEROUS

Blanche Mackey

Lee Child has been a television director, union organizer, theater technician, and law student. He is the author of the Jack Reacher novels. He was born in England but now lives in New York City and leaves the island of Manhattan only when required to by forces beyond his control. Visit www.leechild.com for more information on his books, short stories, and the *Jack Reacher* movie starring Tom Cruise.

my first drug trial
by lee child

Was it smart to smoke a bowl before heading to court? Probably not. The charge was possession of a major quantity, and first impressions count, and a courtroom is a theater with all eyes on just two main characters: the judge, obviously, but mostly the accused. So was it smart?

Probably not.

But what choice did I have? Obviously I had smoked a bowl the night before. A big bowl, to be honest. Because I was nervous. I wouldn't have slept without it. Not that I have tried to sleep without it, even one night in twenty years. So that hit was routine. I slept the sleep of the deeply stoned and woke up feeling normal. And looking and acting normal, I'm sure. At breakfast my wife made no adverse comment, except, "Use some Visine, honey." But it was said with no real concern. Like advice about which tie to choose. Which I was happy to have. It was a big day for me, obviously.

So I shaved and dripped the drops into my eyes, and then I showered, which on that day I found especially symbolic. Even transformational. I felt like I was hosing a waxy residue that only I could see out of my hair and off my skin. It sluiced away down the drain and left me feeling fresh and clean. A new man, again. An innocent man. I stood in the warm stream for an extra minute and for the millionth time half-decided to quit. Grass is not addictive. No physical component. All within my power. And I knew I should.

That feeling lasted until I had finished combing my hair. The light in my bathroom looked cold and dull. The plain old day bore down on me. Problem is, when you've stayed at the Ritz, you don't want to go back to the Holiday Inn.

I had an hour to spare. Courts never start early. I had set the time aside to review some issues. You can't expect lawyers to spot everything. A man has to take responsibility. So I went to my study. There was a pipe on the desk. It was mostly blackened, but there were some unburned crumbs.

I opened the first file. They had given me copies of everything, of course. All the discovery materials. All the pleadings and the depositions and the witnesses. I was familiar with the facts, naturally. And objectively, they didn't look good. Any blow-dried TV analyst would sit there and say, *Things don't look good here for the accused.* But there were possibilities. Somewhere. There had to be. How many things go exactly to plan?

The unburned crumbs were fat and round. There was a lighter in the drawer. I knew that. A yellow plastic thing from a gas station. I couldn't concentrate. Not properly. Not in the way I needed to. I needed that special elevated state I knew so well. And it was within easy reach.

Irresponsible, to be high at my first drug trial.

Irresponsible, to prepare while I was feeling less than my best.

Right?

I held the crumbs in with my pinkie fingernail and knocked some ash out around it. I thumbed the lighter. The smoke tasted dry and stale. I held it in, and waited, and waited, and then the buzz was there. Just microscopically. I felt the tiny thrills, in my chest first, near my lungs. I felt each cell in my body flutter and swell. I felt the light brighten and I felt my head clear.

Unburned crumbs. Nothing should be wasted. That would be criminal.

The blow-dried analysts would say the weakness in the prosecution's case was the lab report on the substances seized. But weakness was a relative word. They would be expecting a conviction.

They would say the weakness in the defense's case was all of it.

No point in reading more.

It was a railroad, straight and true.

Nothing to do for the balance of the morning hour.

I put the pipe back on the desk. There were paperclips in a drawer. Behind me on a shelf was a china jar marked *Stash*. My brother had bought it for me. Irony, I suppose. In it was a baggie full of Long Island grass. Grown from seeds out of Amsterdam, in an abandoned potato field close enough to a bunch of Hamptons mansions to deter police helicopters. Rich guys don't like noise, unless they're making it.

I took a paperclip from the drawer and unbent it and used it to clean the bowl. Just housekeeping at that point. Like loading the dishwasher. You have to keep on top of the small tasks. I made a tiny conical heap of ash and carbon on a tissue, and then I balled up the tissue and dropped it in the trash basket. I blew through the pipe, hard, like a pygmy warrior in the jungle. Final powdered fragments came out, and floated, and settled.

Clean.

Ready to go.

For later, of course. Because right then those old unburned crumbs were doing their job. I was an inch off the ground, feeling pretty good. For the moment. In an hour I would be sliding back to earth. Good timing. I would be clear of eye and straight of back, ready for whatever the day threw at me.

But it was going to be a long day. No doubt about that. A long, hard, pressured, unaided, uncompensated day. And there was nothing I could do about it. Not even I was dumb enough to show up at a possession trial with a baggie in my pocket. Not that there was anywhere to smoke anymore. Not in a public facility. All part of the collapse of society. No goodwill, no convenience. No joy.

I swiveled my chair and scooted toward the shelf with the jar. Just for a look. Like a promise to myself that the Ritz would be waiting for me after the day in the Holiday Inn. I took off the lid and pulled out the baggie and shook it uncrumpled. Dull green, shading brown, dry and slightly crisp. Ready for instantaneous combustion. A harsher taste that way, in my experience, but faster delivery. And time was going to count.

I decided to load the pipe there and then. So it would be ready for later. No delay. In the door, spark the lighter, relief. Timing was everything. I crumbled the bud and packed the bowl and tamped it down. I put it on the desk and licked my fingers.

Timing was everything. Granted, I shouldn't be high in court. Understood. Although how would people tell? I wasn't going to have much of a role. Not on the first day, anyway. They would all look at me from time to time, but that was all. But it was better to play it safe, agreed. But it was the gap I was worried about. The unburned crumbs were going to give it up long before I arrived downtown. Which was inefficient. Who wants twenty more minutes of misery than strictly necessary?

I picked up the lighter. No one in the world knows more than I do about how a good bud burns. The flame licks over the top layer, and it browns and blackens, and you breathe right in and hold, hold, hold, and the bud goes out again, and you hold some more, and you breathe out, and the hit is there. And you've still got ninety percent left in the bowl, untouched, just lightly seasoned. Maybe ninety-five percent. Hardly like smoking at all. Just one pass with the lighter. Merely a gesture.

And without that gesture, twenty more minutes of misery than strictly necessary.

What's a man supposed to do?

I sparked the lighter. I made the pass. I held the smoke deep inside, harsh and hot and comforting.

My wife came in.

"Jesus," she said. "Today of all days?"

So it was her fault, really. I breathed out too soon. I didn't get full value. I said, "No big deal."

"You're an addict."

"It's not addictive."

"Emotionally," she said. "Psychologically."

Which was a woman thing, I supposed. A man has a stone in his shoe, he takes it out, right? Who walks around all day with a stone in his shoe? I said, "Nothing's going to happen for an hour or so."

She said, "You can't afford to fall asleep. You can't afford to look all spacey. You understand that, right? Please tell me you understand that."

"It was nothing," I said.

"There will be consequences," she said. "We're doing well right now. We can't afford to lose it all."

"I agree, we're doing well. We've always done well. So don't worry."

"Today of all days," she said again.

"It was nothing," I said again. I held out the pipe. "Take a look."

She took a look. Exactly as predicted. The top layer a little burned, the rest untouched but lightly seasoned. Ninety-five percent still there. A breath of fresh air. Hardly like smoking at all.

She said, "No more, okay?"

Which I absolutely would have adhered to, except she had made me waste the first precious moment. And I wanted to time it right. That was all. No more and no less. I wanted to be ready when the fat guy in the uniform called out, *All rise!* But not before. No point in being ready before. No point at all.

My wife spent a hard minute looking at me, and then she left the room again. The car service was due in about twenty minutes. The ride downtown would take another twenty. Plus another twenty milling around before we all got down to business. Total of an hour. The aborted breath would have seen me through. I was sure of that. So one more would replace it. Maybe a slightly smaller version, to account for the brief passage of time. Or maybe a slightly larger version, to compensate for the brief upset. I had been knocked off my stride. Ritual is important, and interference can be disproportionately destructive.

I sparked up again. The yellow lighter. A yellow flame, hot and pure and steady. Problem is, the second pass burns better. As if those lower seasoned layers are ready and waiting. They know their fate, and they're instantly ready to cooperate. Smoke came up in a cloud, and I had to breathe in hard to capture all of it. And second time around the bud doesn't extinguish quite so fast. It keeps on smoldering, so a second breath is necessary. Waste not, want not.

Then a third breath.

By which time I knew I was right. I was getting through the morning just fine. I had saved the day. No danger of getting sleepy. I wasn't going to look spacey. I was bright, alert, buzzing, seeing things for what they were, open to everything, magical.

I took a fourth breath, which involved the lighter again. The smoke was gray and thick and instantly satisfying. I could feel the roots of my hair growing. The follicles were thrashing with microscopic activity. I could hear my neighbors getting ready for work. Stark and absolute clarity everywhere. My spine felt like steel, warm and straight and unbending, with brain commands rushing up and down its mysterious tubular interior, fast, precise, logical, targeted.

I was *functioning*.

Functioning just *fine*.

A fourth hit, and a fifth. There was a lot of weed in the bowl. I had packed it pretty tight. A homecoming treat, remember? That had been the intention. Not really a wake-and-bake. But it was there.

So I smoked it.

I felt good in the car. How could I not? I was ready to beat the world. And capable of it. The traffic seemed to get out of the way, and all the lights were green. Whatever it takes, baby. A guy should always max himself up to the peak of his capabilities. He shortchanges himself any other way. He owes himself and the world his best face, and how he gets it is his own business.

They took me in through a private door, because the public lobby was a zoo. My heels tapped on the tile, fast and rhythmic and authoritative. I was standing straight and my shoulders were back. They made me wait in a room. I could hear the crowd through the door. A low, tense buzz. They were all waiting for my entrance. Hundreds of eyes, waiting to move my way.

"Time," someone said.

I pushed open the door into the well of the court. I saw the lawyers, and the spectators, and the jury pool. I saw the defendant at his table. The fat guy in the uniform called out, "All rise!"

Charles Gross

Joyce Carol Oates is the author most recently of the novels *Mudwoman* and *Daddy Love,* and the story collections *Black Dahlia & White Rose* and *The Corn Maiden & Other Stories.* She has appeared in a number of mystery/suspense anthologies, including *The Best American Mystery Stories of the 20th Century* and *The Dark End of the Street* edited by Jonathan Santlofer and S.J. Rozan. Her next novel is the Gothic mystery *The Accursed.* She is a recipient of the National Book Award, the National Book Critics Circle Lifetime Achievement Award, and the National Medal in the Humanities.

high
by joyce carol oates

How much? she was asking.

For she knew: she was being exploited.

Her age. Her naïveté. Her uneasiness. Her good tasteful expensive clothes. Her *hat*.

Over her shimmering silver hair, a black cloche cashmere *hat.*

And it was the wrong part of town. For a woman like her.

How much? she asked, and when she was told she understood that yes, she was being exploited. No other customers on this rainy weekday night in the vicinity of the boarded-up train depot would pay so much. She was being laughed at. She was being eyed. She was being assessed. It was being gauged of her—*Could we take all her money, could we take her car keys and her car, would she dare to report us? Rich bitch*.

She knew. She suspected. She was very frightened but she was very excited. She thought, *I am the person who is here, this must be me. I can do this.*

She paid. Never any doubt but that the silver-haired lady would pay.

And politely she said, for it was her nature to speak in such a way, after any transaction, *Thank you so much!*

Self-medicating, you might call it.

Though she hated the weakness implied in such a term—*medicating!*

She wasn't desperate. She wasn't a careless, reckless, or stupid woman. If she had a weakness it was being suffused with *hope.*

I need to save myself. I don't want to die.

Her hair! Her hair had turned, not overnight, but over a period of several distraught months, a luminous silver that, falling to her shoulders, parted in the center of her head, caused strangers to stare after her.

Ever more beautiful she was becoming. Elegant, ethereal.

After his death she'd lost more than twenty pounds.

His death she carried with her. For it was precious to her. Yet awkward like an oversized package in her arms she dared not set down anywhere.

Almost, you could see it—the bulky thing in her arms.

Almost, you wanted to flee from her—the bulky thing in her arms was a terrible sight.

I will do this, she said. *I will begin.*

She'd never been "high" in her life. She'd never smoked marijuana—which her classmates had called *pot, grass, dope.* She'd been a good girl. She'd been a cautious girl. She'd been a reliable girl. In school she'd had many friends—the safe sort of friends. They hadn't been careless, reckless, or stupid, and they'd impressed their influential elders. They'd never gotten *high* and they had passed into adulthood successfully and now it was their time to begin *passing away.*

She thought, *I will get high now. It will save me.*

The first time, she hadn't needed to leave her house. Her sister's younger daughter Kelsey came over with another girl and an older boy of about twenty, bony-faced, named Triste (Agnes thought this was the name: "Triste"), who'd provided the marijuana.

Like this, they said. *Hold the joint like this, inhale slowly, don't exhale too fast, keep it in.*

They were edgy, loud-laughing. She had to suppose they were laughing at her.

But not mean-laughing. She didn't think so.

Just, the situation was *funny*. Kids their age, kids who smoked dope, weren't in school and weren't obsessing about the future, to them the lives of their elders just naturally seemed *funny*.

Kelsey wasn't Agnes's favorite niece. But the others—nieces, nephews—were away at college, or working.

Kelsey was the one who hadn't gone to college. Kelsey was the one who'd been in rehab for something much stronger than marijuana—OxyContin, maybe. And the girl's friends had been arrested for drug possession. Her sister had said, *Kelsey has broken my heart. But I can't let her know*.

Agnes wasn't thinking of this. Agnes was thinking, *I am a widow, my heart has been broken. But I am still alive.*

Whatever the transaction was, how much the dope had actually cost, Agnes was paying, handing over bills to Triste who grunted, shoving them into his pocket. Agnes was feeling grateful, generous. Thinking how long it had been since young people had been in her house, how long even before her husband had died, how long since voices had been raised like this and she'd heard laughter.

They'd seemed already high, entering her house. And soon there came another, older boy, in his mid-twenties perhaps, with a quasi-beard on his jutting jaw, in black T-shirt, much-laundered jeans, biker boots, forearms covered in lurid tattoos.

"Hi there, Aggie. How's it goin'!"

Agnes, she explained. Her name was *Agnes.*

The boy stared at her. Not a boy but a man in his early thirties, in the costume of a boy. Slowly he smiled as if she'd said something witty. He'd pulled into her driveway in a rattly pickup.

"*Ag-nez.* Cool."

They'd told him about her, maybe. They felt sorry for her and were protective of her.

Her shoulder-length silvery hair, her soft-spoken manner.

The expensive house, like something in a glossy magazine. That she was Kelsey's actual aunt, and a *widow*.

The acquisition of a "controlled substance"—other than prescription drugs—was a mystery to Agnes, though she understood that countless individuals, of all ages but primarily young, acquired these substances easily: marijuana, cocaine, amphetamines, OxyContin, Vicodin, even heroin and "meth." *Self-medicating* had become nearly as common as aspirin. *Recreational drugs* began in middle school.

She was a university professor. She understood, if not in precise detail, the undergraduate culture of alcohol, drugs.

These were not university students, however. Though her niece Kelsey was enrolled in a community college.

Like this, Aunt Agnes.

It was sweet, they called her Aunt Agnes, following Kelsey's lead. She liked being an *aunt*. She had not been a *mother*.

They passed the joint to her. With shaky fingers she held the stubby cigarette to her lips—drew the acrid smoke into her lungs—held her breath for as long as she could before coughing.

She'd never smoked tobacco. She'd been careful of her health. Her husband, too, had been careful of his health: he'd exercised, ate moderately, drank infrequently. He'd smoked, long ago—not for thirty years. But then, he'd been diagnosed with lung cancer and rapidly it had metastasized and within a few months he was gone.

Gone was Agnes's way of explanation. *Dead* she could not force herself to think, let alone speak.

Kelsey was a good girl, Agnes was thinking. She'd had some trouble in high school but essentially, she was a good girl. After rehab she'd begun to take courses at the community college—computer science, communication skills. Agnes's sister had said that Kelsey was the smartest of her children, and yet—

Silver piercings in her face glittered like mica. Her mouth was dark purple like mashed grapes. It was distracting to Agnes, how her niece's young breasts hung loose in a low-slung, soft jersey top thin as a camisole.

She brought the joint to her lips, that felt dry. Her mouth filled with smoke—her lungs.

He'd died of lung cancer. So unfair, he had not smoked in more than thirty years.

Yet individuals who'd never smoked could get lung cancer, and could die of lung cancer. In this matter of life and death, the notion of *fair, unfair* was futile.

"Hey, Auntie Agnes! How're you feelin'?"

She said she was feeling a little strange. She said it was like wine—except different. She didn't feel *drunk*.

Auntie they were calling her. Affectionately, she wanted to think—not mockingly.

So strange, these young people in her house! And her husband didn't seem to be here.

Strange, every day that he wasn't here. That fact she could contemplate for long hours like staring at an enormous boulder that will never move.

Strange, too, she remained. *She* had not died—had she?

There was her niece Kelsey and there was Kelsey's friend Randi, and bony-faced Triste, and—was it Mallory, with the tattoos? She wasn't sure. She was feeling warm, a suffusion of warmth in the region of her heart. She was laughing now, and coughing. Tears stung her eyes. Yet she was *not sad*. These were tears of happiness not sadness. She felt—expansive? elated? excited? Like walking across a narrow plank over an abyss.

If the plank were flat on the ground, you would not hesitate. You would smile, this crossing is so easy.

But if the plank is over an abyss, you feel panic. You can't stop yourself from looking down, into the abyss.

Don't look. Don't look. Don't look.

Her young friends were watching her, and laughing with her. A silvery-haired woman of some unfathomable age beyond sixty in elegant clothes, rings on her fingers, sucking at a joint like a middle school kid. *Funny!*

Or maybe, as they might say, *weird.*

How long the young people stayed in her house Agnes wouldn't know. They were playing music—they'd turned on Agnes's radio, and tuned it to an AM rock station. The volume so high, Agnes felt the air vibrate. She had to resist the impulse to press her hands over her ears. Her young friends were laughing, rowdy. Kelsey was holding her hand and calling her *Auntie*. It was a TV comedy—brightly lit, and no shadows. Except she'd become sleepy suddenly. Barely able to walk, to climb the stairs, Kelsey and another girl had helped her. Someone's arm around her waist so hard it hurt.

"Hey, Aunt Agnes, are you okay? Just lay down, you'll feel better."

Kelsey was embarrassed for her widow-aunt. Or maybe—Kelsey was amused.

She was crying now. Or, no—not crying so they could see. She'd learned another kind of crying that was *inward, secret.*

Kelsey helped her lie on her bed, removed her shoes. Kelsey and the other girl were laughing together. A glimpse of Kelsey holding a filmy negligee against her front, cavorting before a mirror. The other girl, opening a closet door. Then she was alone.

She was awake and yet, strange things were happening in her head. Strange noises, voices, laughter, static. Her husband was knocking at the door which inadvertently she'd locked. She had not meant to lock him out. He was baffled and panicked by the loud music in his house. Yet she was paralyzed and could not rise from her bed to open the door. *Forgive me! Don't go away, I love you.*

After a while it was quiet downstairs.

* * *

In the morning she woke to discover the lights still on downstairs and the rooms ransacked.

Ransacked was the word her husband would use. *Ransacked* was the appropriate word for the thievery had been random and careless, as children might do.

Missing were silver candlestick holders, silverware and crystal bowls, her husband's laptop from his study. Drawers in her husband's desk had been yanked open, someone had rummaged through his files and papers but carelessly, letting everything fall to the floor.

A small clock, encased in crystal, rimmed in gold, which had been awarded to her husband for one of his history books, and had been kept on the windowsill in front of her husband's desk, was missing.

A rear door was ajar. The house was permeated with cold. In a state of shock Agnes walked through the rooms. She found herself in the same room, repeatedly. As in a troubled dream, she was being made to identify what had been taken from her.

Yet what the eye does not *see,* the brain can't register. The effort of remembering was exhausting. Her head was pounding. Her eyes ached. Her throat was dry and acrid and the inside of her mouth tasted of ashes.

They hadn't ransacked the upstairs. They hadn't found her purse, her wallet and credit cards. They'd respected the privacy of her bedroom . . .

She had no reason to think that her niece had been involved.

Maybe Kelsey had tried to stop them. But Triste and Mallory had threatened her.

Agnes would never know. She could never ask. She tried to tell herself, *It doesn't mean anything—that she doesn't love me. It means only that they were desperate for money.*

Yet she called her sister to ask for Kelsey. Coolly her sister said that Kelsey didn't live with them any longer, Agnes must know this.

Where did Kelsey live? So far as anyone knew, she lived with "friends."

Kelsey was no longer attending the community college. Agnes must know this.

Bitterly her sister spoke. Though relenting then, realizing it was Agnes, the widowed older sister, to whom she was speaking, and asking why she wanted to speak with Kelsey.

"No reason," Agnes said. "I'm sorry to bother you."

It was terrifying to her, she would probably never see her niece again.

Yet I still love her.

What was exhausting, when she wasn't "high"—she had to plead for her husband's life.

Hours of each day. And through the night pleading, *No! Not ever.*

Not ever give up, I beg you.

As soon as the diagnosis was made, the doctors had given up on him. So it seemed to the stricken wife.

Repeating their calm rote words: *Do you want extraordinary measures taken to sustain your life, in case complications arise during or after surgery?* And her husband who was the kindest of men, the most accommodating and least assertive of men, a gentle man, a thoughtful man, a reasonable man, one who would hide his own anxiety and terror in the hope of shielding his wife, had said quietly what the doctor had seemed to be urging him to say: *No, of course not, doctor. Use your own judgment please.* For this was the brave response. This was the noble response. This was the manly common sense response. In mounting disbelief and horror Agnes had listened to this exchange and dared to interrupt, *No—we're not going to give up. We do want "extraordinary measures"—I want "extraordinary measures" for my husband! Please! Anything you can do, doctor.*

She would beg. She would plead. Unlike her beloved husband she could not be stoic in the face of (his) death.

Yet, in the end, fairly quickly there'd been not much the doctors could do. Her husband's life from that hour onward had gone—had departed—swiftly like thread on a bobbin that goes ever more swiftly as it is depleted.

I love you—so many times she told him. Clutching at him with cold frightened fingers.

Love love love you, please don't leave me.

She missed him so much. She could not believe that he would not return to their house. It was that simple.

In the marijuana haze, she'd half-believed—she'd been virtually certain—that her husband was still in the hospital, and wondering why she hadn't come to visit. Or maybe it was in the dream—the dreams—that followed. *High, I was so high. The earth was a luminous globe below me and above me—there was nothing . . .*

After he'd died, within hours when she returned to the suddenly cavernous house she'd gone immediately to a medicine cabinet and on the spotless white-marble rim above the sink she had set out pills, capsules—these were sleeping pills, painkillers, antibiotics—that had accumulated over a period of years; prescriptions in both her husband's and her name, long forgotten. *Self-medicating*—yet how much more tempting, to *self-erase?*

There were dozens of pills here. Just a handful, swallowed down with wine or whiskey, and she'd never wake again—perhaps.

"Should I? Should I join you?"—it was ridiculous for the widow to speak aloud in the empty house, yet it seemed to her the most natural thing in the world; and what was unnatural was her husband's failure to respond.

She would reason, *It's too soon. He doesn't understand what has happened to him yet.*

Weeks now and she hadn't put the pills away. They remained on the marble ledge. Involuntarily her eye counted them—five, eight, twelve, fifteen—twenty-five, thirty-five . . .

She wondered how many sleeping pills, for instance, would be "fatal." She wondered if taking too many pills would produce nausea and vomiting; taking too few, she might remain semi-conscious, or lapse into a vegetative state.

Men were far more successful in suicide attempts than women. This was generally known. For men were not so reluctant to do violence to their bodies: gunshots, hanging, leaping from heights.

I want to die but not to experience it. I want my death to be ambiguous so people will say—It was an accidental overdose!

So people will say—She would not live without him, this is for the best.

What a relief, that Kelsey and her friends hadn't come up-stairs to steal from her! They'd respected her privacy, she wanted to think.

How stricken with embarrassment she'd have been if Kelsey had looked into the bathroom and seen the pills so openly displayed. Immediately her niece would have known what this meant, and would have called her mother.

Mom! Aunt Agnes is depressed and suicidal—I thought you should know.

At least, Agnes thought that Kelsey might have made this call.

"Zeke! Thank you."

And, "Zeke—how much do I owe you?"

From a young musician friend, a former student, now years since he'd been an undergraduate student, she'd acquired what she believed to be a higher, purer quality of "pot"—she'd been embarrassed to call him, to make the transaction, pure terror at the possibility (of course, it was not a likely possibility) that Zeke was an undercover agent for the local police; she'd encountered him by chance in an organic foods store near the university, he'd been kind to her, asking after her, of course he'd heard that Professor Krauss had died, so very sorry to hear such sad and unexpected news . . . Later she'd called him, set up a meeting at the local mall, in the vast parking lot, she'd been awkward and ashamed and yet determined, laughing so that her face reddened. To Zeke she was Professor Krauss also. To all her admiring students.

A Ziploc bag Zeke sold her. Frankly, he'd seemed surprised—then concerned. He'd been polite as she remembered him, from years ago. She told the ponytailed young man she was having friends over for the evening, friends from graduate-student days, Ann Arbor. He'd seemed to believe her. No normal person would much want to *get high* by herself, after all.

As soon as she was safely home she lit a joint and drew in her breath as Kelsey had taught her—cautiously, but deeply. The heat was distracting. She didn't remember such heat. And the dryness, the acridity. Again she began to cough—tears spilled from her eyes. Her husband had said, *What are you doing, Agnes? Why are you doing such things? Just come to me, that's all. You know that.*

Mattia.

Running her forefinger down the *Mattia* listings. There were a surprising number—at least a dozen. Most young people had cell phones now. The Mercer County, New Jersey phone directory had visibly shrunken. Yet there was a little column of *Mattias* headed by *Mattia, Angelo.*

His first name hadn't been Angelo—she didn't think so.

Maybe—had it been Eduardo?

(There was a listing for *Eduardo*, in Trenton.)

Also listed were *Giovanne, Christopher, Anthony, Thomas, E.L. Mattia . . .*

None of these names seemed quite right to her. Yet she had to suppose that her former student, an inmate-student at East Jersey State Prison (formerly Rahway State Prison), was related to one or more of these individuals.

Impulsively she called the listing for *Mattia, Eduardo*.

If there is no answer, then it isn't meant to happen.

The phone rang at the other end. But no one picked up. A recording clicked on—a man's heavily accented voice—quickly Agnes hung up.

Later, she returned to discover the phone directory which she'd left on a kitchen counter, open to the *Mattia* listings. She stared at the column of names. She thought—*Was the name Joseph?*

It had been a traditional name, with religious associations. A formal name. When Agnes had addressed the young man it was formally, respectfully—*Mr. Mattia.*

Other instructors in the prison literacy program called students by their first names. But not Agnes, who'd taken seriously the program organizer's warning not to suggest or establish any sort of "inappropriate intimacy" with the inmate-students.

Never touch an inmate. Not even a light tap on the arm.

Never reveal your last name to them. Or where you live, or if you are married.

Agnes remembered the eagerness with which she'd read Mattia's prose pieces in her remedial English composition class at the prison several years before. The teaching experience, for her, in the maximum-security state prison, had been exhausting, but thrilling.

A civic-minded colleague at the university had recruited Agnes, who'd been doubtful at first. And Agnes's husband, who thought that prison education was a very good thing, was yet doubtful that Agnes should volunteer. Her training was in Renaissance literature—she'd never taught disadvantaged students of any kind.

She'd told her husband that she would quit the program if she felt uncomfortable. If it seemed in any way risky, dangerous. But she was determined not to be discouraged and not to drop out. In her vanity, she did not wish to think of herself as *weak, coddled*.

Her university students were almost uniformly excellent, and motivated. For she and her historian-husband taught at a prestigious private university. She'd never taught difficult students, public school students, remedial students, or students in any way disabled or "challenged." At this time she was fifty-three years old and looking much younger, slender, with wavy mahogany-dark hair to her shoulders, and a quick friendly smile to put strangers at ease. She'd done volunteer work mostly for Planned Parenthood and for political campaigns, to help liberal Democrats get elected. She had never visited a prison, even a women's detention facility. She'd learned belatedly that her prison teaching was limited to male inmates.

Of her eleven students, eight were African American; two were "white"; and one was *Mattia, Joseph* (she was certain now, the name had had an old-world religious association), who had olive-dark skin with dark eyes, wiry black hair, an aquiline nose, a small neatly trimmed mustache. Like his larger and more burly fellow inmates, Mattia was physically impressive: his shoulders and chest hard-muscled, his neck unusually thick, for one with a relatively slender build. (Clearly, Mattia worked with weights.) Unlike the others he moved gracefully, like an athlete-dancer. He was about five feet eight—inches shorter than the majority of the others.

In the prison classroom Agnes had found herself watching Mattia, in his bright-blue uniform, before she'd known his name, struck by his youthful enthusiasm and energy, the *radiance* of his face.

Strange, in a way Mattia was ugly. His features seemed wrongly sized for his angular face. His eyes could be stark, staring. Yet Agnes would come to see him as attractive, even rather beautiful—as others in the classroom sat with dutiful expressions, polite fixed smiles or faces slack with boredom, Mattia's face seemed to glow with an intense inner warmth.

Agnes had supposed that Mattia was—twenty-five? Twenty-six?

The ages of her students ranged from about twenty to forty, so far as she could determine. It would be slightly shocking to Agnes to learn, after the ten-week course ended, that Mattia was thirty-four; that he'd been in this prison for seven years of a fifteen-year sentence for "involuntary manslaughter"; that he'd enrolled in several courses before hers, but had dropped out before completing them.

The dark-eyed young man had been unfailingly polite to Agnes, whose first name the class had been told, but not her last name. *Ms. Agnes* in Mattia's voice was uttered with an air of reverence as if—so Agnes supposed—the inmate-student saw in her qualities that had belonged to his mother, or to another older woman relative; he was courteous, even deferential, as her university students, who took their professors so much more for granted, were not.

Mattia was the most literate writer in the class, as he was the sharpest-witted, and the most alert. His compositions were childlike, earnest. Yet his thoughts seemed overlarge for his brain, and writing with a stubby pencil was a means of relieving pressure in the brain; writing in class, as Agnes sat at the front of the room observing, Mattia hunched over his desk frowning and grimacing in a kind of exquisite pain, as if he were talking to himself.

Sometimes, during class discussion, Agnes saw Mattia looking at her—particularly, at *her*—with a brooding expression, in which there was no recognition; at such times, his face was mask-like and unsmiling, and seemed rather chilling to her. She hadn't known at the time what his prison sentence was for but she'd thought, *He has killed someone. That is the face of a killer.*

But, as if waking from a trance, in the next moment Mattia smiled, and waved his hand for Agnes to call upon him—*Ms. Agnes!*

She loved to hear her name in his velvety voice. She loved to see his eyes light up, and the mask-like killer-face vanish in an instant, as if it had never been.

Instructors in the composition course used an expository writing text that was geared for "remedial" readers yet contained essays, in primer English, on such provocative topics as racial integration, women's rights, gay and lesbian rights, freedom of speech and of the press, "patriotism" and "terrorism." There was a section on the history of the American civil rights movement, and there was a section on the history of Native Americans and "European" conquest. Agnes assigned the least difficult of the essays, to which her students were to respond in compositions of five hundred words or so. *Just write as if you were speaking to the author. You agree, or disagree—just write down your thoughts.*

Most of the students were barely literate. In their separate worlds, inaccessible to their instructor, they were likely individuals who aroused fear in others, or at least apprehension; but in the classroom, they were disadvantaged as overgrown children. Slowly, with care, Agnes went through their compositions line by line for the benefit of the entire class. The inmate-students had ideas, to a degree—but their ability to express themselves in anything other than simple childish expletives was primitive; and their attitude toward Agnes, respectful at first, if guarded, quickly became sullen and resentful. Even when Agnes tried to praise the "strengths" in their writing, they came to distrust her, for the "suggestions" that were sure to come.

Mattia was quick-witted and shrewd, and usually had no difficulty understanding the essays, but his writing was so strangely condensed, Agnes often didn't know what he was trying to say. It was as if the young man was distrustful of speaking outright. He wrote in the idiom of the street but it was a heightened and abbreviated idiom, succinct as code. From time to time Agnes looked up from one of his tortuous compositions thinking, *This is poetry!* When Mattia read his compositions aloud to the class, he read in a way that seemed to convey meaning, yet often the other inmates didn't seem to understand him, either.

She couldn't determine if the other inmates liked Mattia. She couldn't determine if any of the inmates were friends. In the classes, it was common for inmate-students to sit as far apart from one another as they could, including in the corners of the room, since, in their cells, as Agnes's supervisor had told her, they were in constant overly close quarters.

When, in class, Agnes questioned Mattia about the meaning of his sentences (taking care always to be exceedingly considerate and not to appear to be "critical"), Mattia could usually provide the words he'd left out. He seemed not to understand how oblique his meaning was, how baffled the others were.

"We can't read your mind, Joseph"—so Agnes had said.

She'd meant to be playful, and Mattia had looked startled, and then laughed.

"Ms. Agnes, ma'am, that is a damn good thing!"

The rest of the inmate-students laughed with Mattia, several of them quite coarsely. Agnes chose to ignore the moment, and to move on.

During the ten-week course, Mattia was the only student not

to miss a single class, and Mattia was the only student who handed in every assignment. Though she was to tell no one about him, not her supervisor, not her fellow instructors, and not her husband, Agnes was fascinated by this "Joseph Mattia"—not only his writing ability but his personality, and his presence. It had always been deeply satisfying to Agnes to teach her university students, but there was no risk involved, as the university campus represented no risk to enter; there was no prison protocol to be observed; as an Ivy League professor, she knew that if she'd never entered her students' lives, their lives would not be altered much, for they'd been surrounded by first-rate teachers for most of their lives. But at this prison, Ms. Agnes might actually make a difference in an inmate's life, if he allowed it.

Mattia's prose pieces grew more assured with the passage of weeks. He knew Ms. Agnes thought highly of him: she was one of those adults in authority, one of those members of the *white world*, who held him in high esteem, and would write positively and persuasively on his behalf to the parole board.

I am happy to recommend. Without qualification.

One of my very best students in the course. Gracious, courteous, sense of humor. Trustworthy. Reliable.

It was evident from Mattia's oblique prose pieces that he had committed acts of which he was "ashamed"—but Mattia had not been specific, as none of the inmates were specific about the reasons for which they were in the maximum-security prison. Only after the course ended did she learn that Mattia had been indicted on a second-degree murder charge, in the death of a Trenton drug dealer; in plea bargaining negotiations, the charge had been reduced to voluntary manslaughter; finally, to involuntary manslaughter. Instead of twenty years to life for murder, Mattia was serving seven years for manslaughter. Agnes told herself, *Probably he was acting in self-defense. Whoever he killed would have killed him. He is not a "killer."*

Mattia's parole had been approved. On the last class day, Mattia had stood before Agnes to thank her. His lips had trembled. His eyes were awash with tears.

Again she thought, *I remind him of—someone. Someone who'd loved him, whom he had loved.*

From his prose pieces, she knew he lived on Tumbrel Street, Trenton, in a neighborhood only a few blocks from the state capitol rotunda and the Delaware River. This was a part of Trenton through which visitors to the state capitol buildings and the art museum drove without stopping, or avoided altogether by taking Route 29, along the river, into the city. Agnes wondered if he would be returning to this neighborhood; very likely, he had nowhere else to go. How she'd wished she might invite him to visit *her*.

Or arrange for him to live elsewhere. Away from the environment that had led to his incarceration.

Hesitantly, in a lowered voice so the other inmate-students wouldn't hear as they shuffled out of the classroom, Mattia said, "Ms. Agnes, d'you think I could send you things? Things I would write?"

Agnes was deeply touched. She thought, *What is the harm in it? Mattia is not like the others.*

He'd wanted to mail her his "writings," he said. "I never had such a wonderful class, Ms. Agnes. Never learned so much . . ."

Agnes hesitated. She knew the brave generous reckless gesture would be to give Mattia her address, so that he could write to her; but instructors had been warned against establishing such relations outside the prison classroom; even to allow Mattia to know Agnes's last name was considered dangerous.

"If I knew you would read what I write, I would write more—I would write with *hope.*"

Yet still Agnes hesitated. "I—I'm sorry, Joseph. I guess—that isn't such a good idea."

Mattia smiled quickly. If he was deeply disappointed in her, he spared her knowing. "Well, ma'am!—thank you. Like I say, I learn *a lot*. Anyway, I feel like—more *hopeful* now."

Agnes was deeply sorry. Deeply disappointed in herself. Such cowardice!

This was a moment, too, when Agnes might have shaken hands with Mattia, in farewell. (She knew that her male instructors violated protocol on such occasions, shaking hands with inmate-students; she'd seen them.) But Agnes was too cautious, and she was aware of guards standing at the doorway, watching her as well as the inmate-students on this last day of class.

"Thank *you*, Joseph! And good luck."

Now, she would make amends.

Several years had passed. If Mattia still lived in Trenton, it would not be such a violation of prison protocol to contact him—would it?

He'd "paid his debt to society"—as it was said. He was a fellow citizen now. She, his former instructor, did not feel superior to him—in her debilitated state, she felt superior to no one—but she did think that, if he still wanted her advice about writing, or any sort of contact with her as a university professor, she might be able to help him.

What had Mattia said, so poignantly—she had given him *hope*. And from him, perhaps she would acquire *hope*.

She was getting high more frequently. Alone in the cavernous house.

Smoking "pot" was becoming as ritualized to her as having a glass of wine had been for her husband, before every meal. She had sometimes joined him, but usually not—wine made her sleepy, and in the night it gave her a headache, or left her feeling, in the morning, mildly depressed. She knew that alcohol was a depressant to the nervous system and that she must avoid it, like the pills on the marble ledge.

Getting high was a different sensation. *Staying high* was the challenge.

Mattia might be a source of marijuana too. She hadn't thought of this initially, but—yes: probably.

(He'd been incarcerated for killing a drug dealer. It wasn't implausible to assume that he might have dealt in drugs himself.)

(Or, he might have cut himself out from his old life entirely. He might be living now somewhere else.)

(She wasn't sure which she hoped for—only that she wanted very much to see him again, and to make amends for her cowardice.)

Getting high gave her clarity: she planned how she would seek out Joseph Mattia. Shutting her eyes, she rehearsed driving to Trenton, fifteen miles from the village of Quaker Heights; exiting at the State Capitol exit, locating Tumbrel Street . . . None of the Mattias listed in the directory lived on Tumbrel Street in Trenton, but Eduardo Mattia lived on Depot Avenue which was close by Tumbrel (so Agnes had determined from a city map), and there was Anthony Mattia on 7th Street and E.L. Mattia (a woman?) on West State Street, also close by. A large family—the Mattias.

In this neighborhood, she could make inquiries about "Joseph Mattia"—if she dared, she could go to one of the Mattia addresses and introduce herself.

Do you know Joseph Mattia? Is he a relative of yours?

Joseph was a former student of mine who'd been very promising.

Hello! My name is—

Hello! I am a former teacher of Joseph Mattia.

Her heart began pounding quickly, in this fantasy.

Getting high was a dream. *Waking* was the fear.

* * *

In the cavernous house the phone rang frequently. She pressed her hands over her ears.

"Nobody's home! Leave me alone."

She had no obligation to pick up a ringing phone. She had no obligation to return e-mail messages marked *CONCERNED*—or even to read them.

Since getting high she was avoiding relatives, friends. They were dull "straight" people—*getting high* to them meant alcohol, if anything.

Of course they would disapprove of her behavior. Her husband would disapprove. She could not bear them talking about her.

Sometimes the doorbell rang. Upstairs she went to see who it might be, noting the car in the driveway.

These visitors, importunate and "concerned"—she knew she must deflect them, to prevent them calling 911. She would make a telephone call and hurriedly leave a message saying that she was fine but wanted to be alone for a while; or, she would send a flurry of e-mails saying the same thing.

Alone alone alone, she wanted to be alone. Except for Joseph Mattia.

Another time making a purchase from her musician-friend Zeke. And another time. And each time the price was escalating.

The third time, Agnes asked Zeke about this: the price of a Ziploc bag of "joints." And with a shrug Zeke said, "It's the market, Agnes. Supply and demand."

The reply was indifferent, even rude. Zeke did not seem to care about *her.*

She was hurt. She was offended. Didn't he respect Professor Krauss any longer? The way *Agnes* had rolled off his tongue, and not *Professor Krauss*.

She would find someone else to supply her! Nonetheless, on this occasion, she paid.

* * *

Her first drive to Trumbel Street, Trenton. Five months, three weeks, and two days after the call had come from the hospital summoning her, belatedly.

Getting high gave her the courage. Strength flowing through her veins!

In her expansive floating mood she knew to drive slowly—carefully. She smiled to think how embarrassing it would be, to be arrested by police for a DUI—at her age.

In the car she laughed aloud, thinking of this.

The car radio was tuned now to the Trenton AM station. Blasting rap music, rock, high-decibel advertisements. *Fat Joe. Young Jeezy. Ne-Yo. Tyga. Cash Out.* She understood how such sound assailing her ears was an infusion of strength, courage.

Such deafening sound, and little room for fear, caution. Little room for *thought.*

It was *thought* that was the enemy, Agnes understood. Getting high meant rising above *thought.*

She exited Route 1 for the state capitol buildings. Through a circuitous route involving a number of one-way streets and streets barricaded for no evident reason, she made her way to Trumbel Street which was only two blocks from State Street and from the Delaware River. This was a neighborhood of decaying row houses and brownstones—boarded-up and abandoned stores. It was tricky—treacherous!—to drive here, for the narrow streets were made narrower by parked vehicles.

Very few "white" faces here. Agnes was feeling washed-out, anemic.

It was a neighborhood of very dark-skinned African Americans and others who were light-skinned, possibly African American and/or Hispanic. Eagerly she looked for *him*.

Turning onto 7th Street and State Street, which was a major

thoroughfare in Trenton, she saw more "white" faces—and many pedestrians, waiting for buses.

Why did race matter so much? The color of *skin*.

She could love anyone, Agnes thought. Skin color did not mean anything to her, only the soul within.

Mattia's liquid-dark eyes. Fixed upon her.

Ms. Agnes, I feel like—more hopeful now.

A half-hour, forty minutes Agnes drove slowly along the streets of downtown Trenton. Trumbel to West State Street and West State Street to Portage; Portage to Hammond, and Grinnell Park; right turn, and back to Trumbel which was, for a number of blocks, a commercial street of small stores—Korean food market, beauty salon, nail salon, wig shop, diner, tavern. And a number of boarded-up, graffiti-marked stores. Trenton was not an easy city to navigate since most of the streets were one-way. And some were barricaded—under repair. (Except there appeared to be no workers repairing the streets, just abandoned-looking heavy equipment.) She saw men on the street who might have been Joseph Mattia but were not. Yet she felt that she was drawing closer to him.

She told herself, *I have nothing else to do. This is my only hope.*

Her husband would be dismayed! She could hardly bring herself to think of him, how he would feel about her behavior now; how concerned he would be. He'd promised to "protect" her—as a young husband he'd promised many things—but of course he had not been able to protect her from his own mortality. She'd been a girl when he'd met her at the University of Michigan. Her hair dark brown, glossy-brown, and her eyes bright and alert. Now, her hair had turned silver. It was really a remarkable hue, she had only to park her car, to walk along the sidewalk—here, on Trumbel Street—to draw eyes to her, startled and admiring.

Ma'am, you are beautiful!

Whatever age you are, ma'am—you lookin' good.

Ma'am—you someone I know, is you?

These were women mostly. Smiling African American women.

For this walk in Trenton she wore her good clothes. A widow's tasteful clothes, black cashmere. And the cloche hat on her silvery hair. And good shoes—expensive Italian shoes she'd purchased in Rome, the previous summer traveling with her historian-husband.

They'd also gone to Florence, Venice, Milano, Delphi. Her husband had brought along one of his numberless guidebooks—this one titled *Mysteries of Delphi*. She'd been astonished to see, superimposed upon photographs of the great ruined sites, transparencies indicating the richness of color of the original sites—primary colors of red and blue—and extraordinary ornamental detail that suggested human specificity instead of "classic" simplicity. Of course, Agnes should have known, but had never thought until her husband explained to her, that the ancient temples weren't classics of austerity—pearl-colored, luminous, stark—but varicolored, even garish. Ruins had not always been *ruins*. Like most tourists she'd assumed that the ancient sites had always been, in essence, what they were at the present time. Like most tourists she hadn't given much thought to what she was seeing and her ideas were naïve and uninformed. Her husband had said, *The way people actually live is known only to them. They take their daily lives with them, they leave just remnants for historians to decode*.

He had opened that world of the past to her. And now, he himself had become *past*.

She thought, *He took everything with him. No one will remember who he was—or who I was.*

She was beginning to feel very strange. A lowering of blood pressure—she knew the sensation. Several times during the hospital vigil and after his death she'd come close to fainting, and twice she had found herself on the floor, dazed and uncomprehending.

The sensation began with a darkening of vision, as color bleached out of the world; there came then a roaring in her ears, a feeling of utter sorrow, lostness, futility . . .

At the intersection of 7th Street and Hammond, out of a corner bodega he stepped, carrying a six-pack of beer.

He was older, of course. He must have been—nearly forty.

His dark hair threaded with gray was longer than she recalled, his eyes were deep-socketed and red-lidded. His skin seemed darker, as if smudged. And he was wearing civilian clothes, not the bright blue prison uniform that had given to the most hulking inmates a look of clownishness—his clothes were cheaply stylish, a cranberry-colored shirt in a satiny fabric, open at the throat; baggy cargo pants, with deep pockets and a brass-buckle belt riding low on his narrow hips.

She saw, in that instant: the narrowed eyes, the aquiline nose, the small trim mustache on the upper lip. And something new—through his left eyebrow, a wicked little zipperlike scar.

He stopped dead in his tracks. He stared at her, and then very slowly he smiled as a light came up in his eyes, of crafty recollection.

"Ma'am! You lookin' *good.*"

Miggi Hood

Linda Yablonsky is the author of *The Story of Junk: A Novel.* As a journalist and critic, she covers the contemporary art world for *T: The New York Times Style Magazine, Artforum, W, Elle, Wallpaper,* and other publications. Current projects include a memoir of life in New York during the 1970s, and a new novel.

jimmy o'brien
by linda yablonsky

Over the winter of 1980, I caught hepatitis and had to stay home for a month. No drinking, the doctor said. He didn't say anything about smoking pot.

If your thinking tends toward the dark side even when life is sunny, hepatitis can feel like the end of the world. You can't get out of bed. You read depressing books. No one wants to come near you. Not that you want anyone to see you with a pimpled yellow complexion and jaundiced eyes. Then there's the bloat of your belly. That alone can make you want to die. Spoon the pain of inflammation into your cup of humiliation, and you have a flawless recipe for despair.

Jimmy O'Brien was my savior. He nursed me from a safe distance. Five thousand miles, he said. He had left New York and was living on the Big Island in Hawaii, growing Mary Jane. His mother in New Jersey had seen an ad for the land and invested all her savings.

During my illness, his phone calls and the product he sent me, ostensibly to sell, made all the difference. Smoking his weed lifted my spirits. It relieved my discomfort. Watch the mail, he'd say. I'm gonna send you a present.

Jimmy was always nice to me. Up until the time Alice shacked up with him, I thought he was gay. What else was I supposed to think? He was with Johnny Giovanni every time I saw him, and Johnny was undeniably queer. Don't tell my girlfriend, Jimmy would say, but it wasn't an affair. It was theater.

Johnny called himself a "body artist" and Jimmy was his foil. They went around town together just for show. Photographers dove after them. They were both six feet tall and kinky, in a comic sort of way. The fashion crowd adored them. The tabloids reported their escapades. We looked. We lusted. We laughed. *Oh God,* Alice would say. *Who are they?*

Johnny was a prancing spider, thin and swarthy. He cultivated a scruff of beard. On the street, his jacket opened on a bare, buff chest that he shaved and polished. He tied leather straps across it, pulling them taut under his nipples. No matter what the weather, he never wore a shirt. Just quilted black jodhpurs, wraparound shades, and, usually, a skullcap of black leather that was more like a hood. We had mutual friends. They looked after him. He had genuine talent, but he couldn't take care of himself.

Jimmy was an Adonis, an angel cake of manhood, light on his feet. He moved with a swing of his narrow hips and a toss of his long blond hair. It fell past broad, square shoulders as chiseled as his jaw. I could never take my eyes off him. High cheekbones, blue eyes, wide mouth set in a permanent grin, he titillated and growled, he giggled like a girl. He could also pose a threat. Danger lurked in his hands. Hardly an hour would pass without him offering to punch a guy out.

He wore the same outfit day and night: a white T-shirt, black leather pants molded to his muscled body, black leather cuffs, and a black leather jacket that set off the golden rain of his hair. In hot weather he traded the leather pants for jeans just as tight, a Bowie knife tucked in his boot.

We'd meet up at Johnny's for a drink and a toke, and go dancing, except that Jimmy didn't dance. He'd get a drink and rest his head in a woofer, feeling the beat. No music could be loud enough.

Jimmy always had his ear to something. A telephone, mostly. It's my girlfriend, he'd say as he dialed. It's my bookie. It's my mom. He didn't have a job. His work was being Jimmy.

He lived with the fashion model who supported him. She was often out of town on a shoot or in Europe for the collections. He knew all the models because of her. He liked pretty women. If you saw them passing a joint, chances are they got it from him, along with diet pills, tranquilizers, and cocaine. He always had a roll of cash. He didn't worry. He didn't have to think.

Never take the subway, he said one night when we couldn't find a cab. The subway was beneath him in more ways than one. He was a king.

I saw him eat now and then, usually breakfast at five a.m., after the clubs had closed. Generally, he lived on drugs and drink. His usual routine was to stay up for eight days and then take a day of rest. Alice called him a miracle of modern medicine. Her father was a doctor and after he met Jimmy he said the same thing.

Alice was divorced. She lived in a suite of rooms on the second floor of her father's sprawling duplex on the Upper West Side, on the park. She kept a full bar in her sitting room. She had cable TV long before the rest of us. Her mother had been an alcoholic who died young, and Alice was moving in the same direction. She worked in a boutique off Fifth Avenue, modeling swimsuits and designing displays. One afternoon, Jimmy stopped by with a bottle of champagne. The sales staff gathered around him with the customers in the store. When the boss arrived, Alice was fired. Jimmy was her consolation.

He's been here for three days, she said, when I went to see her. They hadn't slept at all. She was sitting on her bed, doing her nails. Heavy chains were nailed to the wall above. Leather cuffs dangled from the chains.

Jimmy wasn't just the best sex she had ever had, he was the

best fun. I can't describe it, she said. Bondage appealed to her. Something about the resistance, she said, nodding toward the cuffs. The friction. The harder he pulled the more she wanted him. They fucked all day, all night. They had takeout. He made phone calls and then they fucked again. Of course, there was booze. Of course, there was pot and cocaine and pills. I've never been so wet, she said. It's heaven.

Alice was my best friend. She was almost as tall as Jimmy, but had dark curly hair and wore exaggerated makeup. When she laughed you could see bubbles in the air. More often she was sad, adrift. She felt like an orphan. In her laugh you felt the depth of her.

Jimmy appeared with a bottle of Johnnie Walker. He downed some pills with it and rolled a joint. It was football season and there was a game on TV that he wanted to watch. The only thing that Jimmy liked better than getting stoned was football. And guns. He collected firearms and subscribed to magazines for enthusiasts. In high school, he'd been the quarterback. His only ambition had been to go pro but something had happened. He'd broken training. He'd gotten a girl pregnant. He'd beaten up the captain of the team, I don't know. He had stories.

Now he was back on the phone. Not to his girlfriend. His bookie. He bet on games and he won the bets, for himself and others. When the game was over, he passed out.

Don't go, Alice said. I don't want to be alone.

Sometimes Jimmy called to complain about his girlfriend or Johnny. I don't know how they met. Johnny got on his nerves. He repeated everything he said and needed constant attention. Sometimes Jimmy called to buy weed. I always had a connection. One day he invited me over to his place. His girlfriend was at work and he wanted to play.

I lived in the Village. He was in Spanish Harlem. I took the subway. I had to change trains a few times. It took forever. You gotta get out of that habit, he said. He looked mad.

He had a one-bedroom on the eighth floor. He poured me a cup of coffee and locked himself in the bathroom. Excuse me, he said. I gotta go shoot up.

What a joker. I laughed. And I waited. I sat on the leather couch in his living room, thumbing through the gun and fashion magazines on the coffee table. Thirty minutes later, he emerged in full makeup and a dress.

Am I gorgeous or what? he said, sashaying across the room, a hand on one hip then the other. His gravelly voice had become a breathy falsetto. He ran his tongue over his lips. Think I could get a guy to pick me up in a bar? he twittered. I could go for some handsome devil in a suit.

His slinky blue frock clung to his body, which suddenly seemed curvaceous. The slender legs were good and he walked in his girlfriend's gold heels as if born to them. I took out my lipstick and applied it, partly in self-defense.

You ought to be a model, I said.

I know, he replied. I'm wasting my time taking bets. C'mon, he said. Come out with me. Let's see if we can pick up a couple of jocks!

There was a mirror on the wall and he checked himself out in it. Did his girlfriend know?

Don't you breathe a word, he barked. She hates when I wear her clothes. But see? They fit me better.

I couldn't say. I'd never met her. I was thinking of Alice. His eyes met mine and fluttered. He asked for help with his zipper.

He was naked beneath the dress.

Jimmy wasn't hugely endowed, considering the rest of him. It didn't matter.

Let's go watch the game, he said, and led me into the bedroom. The bed was large and had a steel frame. Its white satin sheets glowed in the waning sunlight from the windows. He closed the blinds and turned on the TV at the foot of the bed. Under it was a large black suitcase. He opened it. Don't peek, he said. When I looked up, he was holding two sets of leather cuffs on short lengths of chain.

Jimmy's tongue filled my mouth and I didn't resist. I was stoned and feeling amorous. He undressed me. Take a breath, he said, attaching a metal clip to each of my nipples and screwing them tight.

That hurts, I said at the pinch. I was surprised by how much it excited me.

Lie down, he said, and I did. He cuffed my wrists and ankles, and hooked the chains to the bed. A flame of desire leapt through my body from my toes to my eyes. They were burning. I opened my legs. I needed air.

I knew you'd like this, he said. He turned on the television. He rolled a joint.

Jimmy!

Don't rush me, he said, and busied his hands in the suitcase. Blood rushed into my ears. I was throbbing. He lit the joint and took a deep toke. Watch the game, he said. Relax.

How does anyone fall in love? I couldn't guess. I thought about money. Money was something you could measure and count. It added up to something. Love was intangible and confusing, impossible to manufacture or predict. Escaping it had more pitfalls than embracing it.

Jimmy!

He put tape on my mouth. He sat down to watch the game. I heard the sound of a crowd cheering, of helmets cracking, men grunting. He turned back and held himself over me, caressing me with his hair and licking me. He tightened the screws and I bucked. He was hard. You look beautiful, he said, and kissed me again. His mouth was soft and his tongue was long. What was I doing? Most of the time, I preferred women to men. But they weren't Jimmy.

He reached into the suitcase.

Fuck me, I said.

He stood up. Now he was holding a shotgun and jerking off. I can't fuck you, he said. My girlfriend would kill me. She'd cut off my hair! She'd dismember me.

The gun went off. I felt the bullet rush past my ear. It hit the pillow inches from my head. You weren't worried, were you? he said. C'mon, let me teach you how to shoot.

He released me and slipped back into the dress. He showed me how to hold the gun, click the safety, how to take the gun apart and clean it, how to put it together again. He stood behind me to guide my aim. The gun had a telescopic sight. We were standing by the bedroom window, looking at a man on the roof of a building across the street.

Get that dweeb, he said. Let me know when you're ready.

I wanted badly to pull that trigger, but not at a total stranger. All that provocation. It got to me.

I'm ready, I said.

That was the last time I saw Jimmy. He called a month later. He was moving to Hawaii, where he was going to get rich growing pot. He was leaving for the good life. He would call. Don't forget me, he said. And stay out of the subway.

For a while, he called every week. The land was fertile and the sensemilla was prime. He still wasn't sleeping. Poachers kept him awake. He shot them. Police helicopters flew overhead. It wasn't the life he expected. But he was determined to stick it out. Once you go a certain distance, there's no turning back.

On my worst day of the hepatitis, the mailman brought a cardboard box postmarked Hawaii. Some books for you, he said. The box was filled with plastic sandwich bags of Jimmy's marijuana, his fat, perfect buds, very clean, very sweet. There was an envelope in the box. Inside it was a Polaroid of Jimmy. He was dressed in a tank top and grinning at the camera. He had a rifle on his shoulder, poking through his hair. I could see mountains behind him and the sky. On the back of the picture it said, *How do I look?*

After that, we lost touch. People come, people go. They cross your path and alter it. There's no turning back.

Life grew more complicated. I no longer lived alone. I quit drinking and smoking pot. It bored me. I hated the smell. Twenty years was enough. My relationship ended. I changed my look. I never thought about Jimmy. Until he phoned, out of the blue, an epoch or so later.

Hey, it's Jimmy! Remember me?

What, you kidding? Jimmy!

He was back in New Jersey, in the town where he grew up. He was a family man, married, two kids. He even had a job coaching high school football. Yeah, he said. White picket fence. The whole nine yards.

He wanted to come into the city. He was clean now, he said, but he still had his weed.

Alice was gone, I told him. Breast cancer. Johnny, his brain exploded. That's all I knew.

I heard, Jimmy said. But you sound good.

I'm good, I said. Call anytime.

He never did.

Jonathan Santlofer is the author of five novels, including *The Death Artist* and *Anatomy of Fear*. He is the recipient of a Nero Award, two NEA grants, has been a visiting artist at the American Academy in Rome, and serves on the board of Yaddo. He is coeditor, contributor, and illustrator of the anthology *The Dark End of the Street,* and editor and contributor of *LA Noire: The Collected Stories,* and Touchstone's serial novel *Inherit the Dead*. Santlofer is director of the Crime Fiction Academy at the Center for Fiction. He lives in Manhattan where he is at work on a new novel.

the last toke
by jonathan santlofer

It's ironic because it all started at a be-in or a love-in, one of those hippy-dippy-paint-your-face-with-flowers events that were so widespread in 1969. This one, on Boston Common, a rare spring day when the sky was painfully blue and everyone was happy or pretending to be, three or four hundred college kids assembled for more than the usual peace and love, a free Tim Hardin concert, blankets on the lawn, jug wine, radios thrumming Mamas & Papas, Beatles, Donovan, Starship, Joan Baez, a folk-rock olio riding the wave of a pot cloud so potent the squirrels were stoned.

My girlfriend had painted flowers on my cheeks and I did the same on hers, petals and stems and leaves, all perfectly delineated and suitable for framing, a competition as we were both art students. My roommate and best friend, Johnny, had rolled a half-dozen joints, something Tim Hardin would appreciate being a junkie and all, though we didn't know that until he OD'd a decade later, my mind a little vague on some details though not others. Tim's first album, mostly melancholy love songs perfect for pseudo-sad college kids, "Don't Make Promises," "It'll Never Happen Again," "How Can We Hang On to a Dream," were filled with palpable despair and words I still know by heart, so it's not true that marijuana will rot your brain as I was smoking it every day at the time.

Tim was an hour and a half late and more than a little fuzzy, forgetting words and once or twice nodding off in mid-song, though we cheered him on the same way I'd cheered on a stumbling-drunk Janis Joplin at Madison Square Garden earlier that year while she lamented her failed love life in between songs and shots of Southern Comfort.

It was later, as we were leaving the concert, all three or four hundred of us pressed together in a throng of impatience that tested our all-you-need-is-love sensibility, when we met the Harvard boys and the older guy, a friend of a friend of a friend, though I never found out whose friend. He was at least thirty, tall and skinny in ratty bellbottoms and a Harry Nilsson T-shirt, and before we made it off the Common he'd asked us (actually he asked my girlfriend) if we wanted to go to a party in Cambridge and she said yes—nobody said no to a party back then.

Cambridge was smarter and savvier than Boston. Boston University students were always a little insecure with the Harvard/Radcliff gang, though as art students we were exempt from academic competition because we didn't take any academics and being art students made us cool by default with our paint-splattered jeans and turpentine cologne. I wore my cool like a Jackson Pollock Halloween costume though deep down I was still a suburban kid who'd let his hair grow and wore John Lennon glasses, twenty years old and about to graduate thinking I knew everything. Oh, if you had seen me with my parents, screaming about capitalism and the war and how money didn't matter and how I was never going to be like them.

The Boston day was slipping toward darkness when we strolled back to BU for my car, a pink Studebaker I'd inherited from my grandfather, mellow on Tim Hardin and grass and cheap wine, face makeup streaked across our cheeks like war paint, me and my girlfriend and Johnny sharing a joint, puffing away in public like we owned Boston, like we owned the world, and we did in the way all twenty-year-olds do with their youth and beauty and audacity.

The Cambridge pad was like so many others, a railroad flat

of endless rooms all reeking of weed and sweat, couples dancing slow to fast music, others dancing alone, a few grinding away, the sexual revolution in full swing.

We'd only been there a few minutes when the older guy offered up some hash. *Got it from a dude who grows it up near Woodstock, powerful stuff*, he said, and after a couple of tokes I knew he was right, cotton batting taking up residence in the crevices of my mind. I was already stoned when he said he had something even better, unwrapping a handkerchief to display what looked like translucent pebbles. *DMT*, he called it. *Like acid, but short and sweet, you only trip for, like, five or ten minutes.*

I was game. So was Johnny, who asked if it was anything like banana peels. The older guy said, *You kidding? Much better than that*, laughed, and dropped a pebble into a hookah and put a match to it, all of us rapt as it flared like a tiny comet.

Johnny took the first inhalation, eyes tearing as he held the smoke in his lungs. Then I took a hit. It smelled like burning metal singeing my nose and throat and then *wham!* my heart was beating like mad, everything starting and stopping, coming and going, the room there and not there, people zooming in and out of focus, George Harrison whine-singing "Within You Without You" deep inside my head, faces around me morphing and melting, apartment walls dissolving into fast-moving clouds like I had been transported into a Magritte painting, and it didn't feel like a few minutes; it felt like forever and a little scary, everything at warp speed.

Then it was over and I was back in the dingy Cambridge apartment, sweating like I had a fever and the older guy was leaning into my girlfriend, the two of them on a mattress covered with a torn Indian blanket, other people on it too but all I could see was them, as if they were in the middle of a fish-eye lens. The older guy placed a joint between her soft lips and looked over at me with a sort of leering smile, then dropped another one of those pebbles into the pipe, and Johnny and I took turns again like trained junkie monkeys and the ceiling exploded and lightning lit up an emerald-green sky and I could feel my heart squishing and squashing, sending blood through my body and I guess I was talking, could hear a kind of slow-motion echo emanating from my mouth but had no idea what I was saying though now the older guy was slapping me on the back and saying, *Thanks, man, thanks,* and the next thing I knew the four of us—me and my girlfriend, Johnny, and the older guy—were piling into my pink Studebaker, windows down, air on my face like a wind tunnel, lightning and comets above us as I drove through Harvard Square, all of us laughing.

At some point I had agreed to help the older guy clean out his apartment though I could not remember when; then my girlfriend said she didn't feel well (an excuse, I was sure) and wanted to go back to the dorm, so we dropped her off but kept going until we were in the suburbs, the whole time the older guy rolling more joints and Johnny and I smoking them, radio blasting Sly and the Family Stone, "Everyday People," and singing along.

Slum-er-ville, the older guy said when we got there. *What everyone calls Somerville, the only place I can afford, with my college loans and all,* a dark street of single and attached houses, none of them nice and not at all like Boston or Cambridge, no streetlights, no charm. *I was a Communications major but can't get a good job so I work part-time for a record producer who fixes me up with cool singers like Grace Slick, who I fucked by the way,* says the older guy, which I did not believe though he went into detail about how Grace smelled and how she talked during sex and how she was from a rich family and how she was kind of a spoiled brat, and then Johnny, always competitive, said, *You wanna hear about the time I fucked Mama Cass?* and he goes right into it.

It was in Monterey, you know, California, and she announces her hotel room from the stage, can you believe that? So I figure what the hell, I go after the show and sure enough there's a bunch of guys hanging in front of her room and finally she comes out, good ol' Mama Cass, I swear to God, all fat and cute in a flowered muumuu, and she crooks a finger at me and says, YOU, *and next thing I know I'm in her room, in her bed, and we're smoking dope and drinking champagne out of the bottle and I'm trying to find her clit, not so easy, heh-heh-heh, and she's telling me what to do and saying what a big cock I have—and I do, man, I really do have a big cock—and I fuck her and she gets off practically screaming and when it's over she asks me if I like her, can you dig it, Mama Cass asking* me *if I like her? I say, sure, sure, of course I like you, and ask if she'll autograph my T-shirt, and she finds her panties and writes on them,* To Johnny with love, from Mama Cass, *and hands them over and I'm like,* Holy shit, right, *so I say,* Hey, will you do me a favor and sing something for me? *and she starts singing, "Dream a Little Dream of Me," but she's changed the words to* Dream a Little Dream of Johnny, *and I swear to God I get goose bumps up and down my arms but I see she's crying, so I ask what's wrong and she says nothing but tells me to go because she's got to get some sleep because they're on the road in the morning, so I fight my way through the crowd of guys still outside her room waving her undies in the air, and they're all hooting and laughing and smacking me on the back and making fat jokes and—*

The older guys sneered and said, *Bullshit*. I backed Johnny up, said I'd seen Mama Cass's large-size autographed undies, which I had not.

Well, she's no Grace Slick, the older guy said, and told me where to park, and we trudged up the stairs of a smallish house to an apartment on the second floor and he's thanking us over and over for helping him and rolls another joint, which we smoked in between regular cigarettes.

Inside, there was hardly any furniture but the living room was a mess of overstuffed Hefty bags and lots of cartons, and the older guy explained he'd just moved in and was still clearing out all the shit left by the former tenants and how he had to get it looking good because his girlfriend from New York was coming to live with him.

I was only half listening, still tripping and a little worried I'd never come out of it, though the older guy assured me it was just an after-effect of the DMT, and thanked me again because he didn't know how he was going to clear out the place without a car and how he couldn't just put all this stuff on the street because the Slumerville garbage collectors wouldn't take it and how his girlfriend was a neat-freak and really beautiful, a model, he said, me thinking he was lying because no way some model was going to go for this scaggy older guy, but he said he was going to marry her even though he didn't believe in marriage, while the three of us started gathering up the Hefty bags and cartons and I explained to the older guy how the Studebaker's seats went all the way down and how it was great for making out but also for fitting in all sorts of junk, and he thanked me again and promised to keep me and Johnny supplied with weed for the rest of our lives.

The older guy said we could leave some of the Hefty bags by the curb, which we did, but not the cartons, which we packed into the Studebaker. When the car was full, I asked, *Now what?* and he said, *Maybe we can find a dump somewhere,* and I said, *Why not just drive around and leave a box here and a box there*? but Johnny came up with the brilliant idea that we dump them into the Charles River, which was exactly what we did with the motorcycle we'd bought earlier in the year, dismantled it and dropped it piece by piece into the river after insuring it with some fly-by-night insurance company, the two of us practically falling down with laughter as we explained that when we tried to collect on our scam it turned out that the fucking insurance company was an even bigger scam and had vanished along with our initial fifty dollars for the phony policy, and how we were so fucked, the older guy shaking his head saying, *You can't trust anyone, especially capitalists.*

So that's what we did, drove around and found secluded spots where we dropped each of his cartons into the murky Charles River.

The older guy thanked us again for saving his life and said we had to meet his model girlfriend sometime and I said, *Sure, sure,* and he offered to buy us beers in a local bar but by then my head felt like someone had tied a string around it and pulled it like a top, it was spinning so bad and Johnny was practically nodding off, so we headed back to BU.

The next day I felt awful, as if someone had taken out my brain, played catch with it, and put it back in, but maybe upside down. I met up with my girlfriend and we went to breakfast at three in the afternoon and after four cups of coffee I could put words together and told her about the older guy and how we helped him with his stuff, and she just shrugged.

That night we went to a party, all art students in an Allston apartment where there was more weed, which I smoked and immediately started tripping, this time coupled with paranoia. I told my girlfriend I had to get out of there but she said no because some graduate art student was going on and on about how painting was dead and that art had to be conceptual and there was no point in making paintings anymore because they had all been made and why add more junk to an already polluted world, and there were a group of undergrads, mostly girls including my girlfriend, literally at his feet looking up at him like he was God.

I left and walked the Allston/Boston streets, angry and paranoid, constantly looking over my shoulder, but eventually found my way home where I lay in bed and stared up at the ceiling, which kept breaking open with dazzling displays of shooting stars, like I had my own private planetarium.

The next day I found out my girlfriend had fucked the "painting is dead" graduate student and we broke up. She went out with him for the rest of the semester, which was only a month or so longer, until he ditched her for a leggy drama student who would later become the movie star Faye Dunaway, and I went off to graduate art school where I stopped smoking pot because I wanted to be a serious artist and pot made me tired and hungry and I was living on Dannon yogurt and Cup O' Noodles and couldn't have afforded pot even if I wanted it.

My ex-girlfriend got in touch with me once and wanted to meet up but I was too proud and stung by her rejection and thought I was pretty cool now that I was a graduate student studying painting and espousing postmodern theory, plus I had started seeing a girl, a sophomore, who thought I was really cool and hung on my every word.

It was about a year after graduate school, when I was playing the life of the artist for real, that I went to the dinner party in Soho, back when Soho was the hip new art scene. There were about a dozen people there, artists and art dealers, a collector or two, and a curator who had just started working at MOMA—someone I clearly wanted to cultivate—and he was saying how he'd gone to Harvard for his masters *and* PhD and I mentioned I was at BU the same years and he didn't make a face when I said it because people in the art world knew BU had a good art school, and he asked me if I was there for the Hansel scandal and I said, *As in Hansel and Gretel*? and a few people laughed but he didn't.

You must have been there when it happened because it was my senior year, which was your senior year, right? Then he stopped, tapped his chin, and said, *Oh, but it didn't come out till the next year so maybe you missed it.*

I said, *Missed what?*

He said, *This guy, Hansel, cut up his girlfriend.*

At that, everyone stopped eating and turned toward him.

Cut her into pieces, he said. *Put her body parts into plastic bags and cartons, which—can you believe?—he dropped into the Charles River!*

I started choking.

Oh, please, said a sophisticated older woman, an art collector wearing a lot of gold jewelry.

It's true, said the Harvard guy, *and he might have gotten away with it but one of the boxes floated up to the surface and some students found it and opened it, and aside from a hand or a foot—I'm pretty sure it was a foot—there was also a letter or a card or something that led the police to him, so he was not only a lunatic but a stupid one, so he must have had help.*

I swallowed hard and said, *Why?*

Well, he didn't have a car and there was no record of a rental.

I said, *Couldn't he have . . . walked?*

The Harvard guy looked at me like I was retarded. *Around the entire Charles River? It would have taken days, weeks. No way. He had help. Someone with a car, the police were sure of it.*

You're quite the expert, I said.

No, though I admit I read everything about it. They never found out who helped him because the guy was dead when the cops discovered him, had been for days, in some awful apartment in Slumerville—that's what everyone in Boston calls Somerville.

I said, *How?*

He said, *How—what?*

How—did he die? My heart was banging against my rib cage like I'd swallowed a live bird.

The host, an artist a few years older, who had been getting attention for his hyperrealistic over-life-size portraits, cut in and asked if anyone wanted to smoke some grass and started passing a joint, and I accepted my first toke in over a year as the Harvard PhD went back to his story.

According to the papers, the killer, a loser who had flunked out of some junior college, Bunker Hill or Roxbury Community, took an overdose of something, plus he was inhaling some sort of hallucinogen that was all the rage that year though I can't remember what it was called.

DMT, I said, not meaning to.

That's it! He looked at me, eyebrows raised, and so did everyone else.

I only tried it once, at a party in Cambridge.

In Cambridge, he said. *Hey, we could have been at the same party!*

Then everyone started asking me questions about DMT like I was a specialist—or a junkie.

Was it like acid?

Was it addictive?

Wasn't it unhealthy?

I dragged on the joint picturing my pink Studebaker filled with boxes of body parts, me and Johnny driving round the Charles River, dropping cartons into murky water and watching them sink while the older guy fed us hash and thanked us over and over for helping him.

Wasn't it dangerous? The sophisticated woman with all the gold jewelry gave me a pointed look.

No, I said, and took one last toke swearing I'd never smoke again. *It only lasted a few minutes. Not enough time to be dangerous.*

PART II

DELIRIUM & HALLUCINATION

Regine Otto-Rodriguez

Abraham Rodriguez was born June 13, 1961 in the South Bronx. From an early age, he showed a big interest in writing, especially on his father's large, clunky typewriters. His father bought him a portable when he was eleven, and from then on he began writing stories and novels. His books include *The Boy without a Flag*, *Spidertown*, *The Buddha Book*, and *South by South Bronx*. His work has appeared in numerous anthologies, including *Bronx Noir* and *The Dark End of the Street*.

moon dust
by abraham rodriguez

I.

Report to Commission C
Inclusions: video files, one (1) short story manuscript
Package of: tainted substance, referred to as "green," "pot," "weed," or, in this case, "Moon Dust"
[WARNING!! DO NOT SMOKE SUBSTANCE.]
Substance will be submitted to the Justice Ministry for examination. It has been weighed and is vigorously controlled. Any misuse will be prosecuted under penal code 717-3 SUPERIOR!!

The sun golden-yellowed over tenement tops.

They were up on the roof, looking down on the apartment. It was a chilly morning, and they both had the collars of their raincoats turned up high.

They were laughing. Bobbing back and forth. They were on a stakeout on a cold morning in the South Bronx. They were freezing their asses off. Their clothes were from the freaking 1890s. They couldn't stop laughing.

"I'm fa-fa-freezing." Killy's teeth chattered.

"It's not even officially fall," Kelly said.

Killy sniffed his own lapel. "Why do we always buy such cheap suits?"

"Uh-uh. I'm not spending money on clothes I'll need just for five minutes someplace. We're doing a lot of time-jumps lately."

"But we'll make ourselves cuh-cuh-conspicuous," Killy said.

"What?!" Kelly stood his six-foot tallness straight, giving Killy an up-and-down look. Black raincoat. Black derby. Killy looked Kelly up-and-down right back. Black raincoat. Black derby. "I think we look quite dapper," Kelly said, lighting an Amnesian stick.

"Hey! Didn't you light an Amnesian stick before we left?"

"I don't remember," Kelly said, and the giggles started for them again.

Killy turned grim. He regarded the stick in his hand. "This is not from this time. We're going to have to smoke it all right now."

"And eat the roach," Kelly said.

A quick couple of tokes for each of them.

Killy went back to his Thermospecs, again sweeping the apartment from one end to the other. Kelly nudged him.

"Hey," he said, "what year is this again?"

This investigation began with a report that there was a "time disturbance" originating in the year 1973 in New York. The disturbance in this case being marijuana tainted with iridium, a substance yet to be discovered. Iridium is the classified substance used in the assembly and successful functioning of the time-sequencer device. We suspect a scientist well-known to this commission, Abraham Ziegler, found a way to somehow break down the active properties of the time portal. To synthesize its elements and somehow compress them into tiny bits. This fine, glittery dust is then sprinkled or sprayed onto marijuana buds.

[See sample. WARNING!! DO NOT SMOKE SUB-STANCE.]

The cumulative effect of smoking the iridium-laced marijuana is limited-experience time travel, "limited" by the amount ingested or smoked. We have as yet acquired no data on duration of the "trips" or what happens when the drug wears off, but we suspect the subject returns back to its own time. This may depend on the amount ingested or smoked.

~

The Thermospecs made a weird whirring sound. Killy scanned the apartment. "I'm seeing four people," he said as he pulled the small gun from an inner pocket. He set the laser sight, and fired. Sounded like sand through a straw. The sonic bomb is about the size of a small kiwi. The term "sonic" is a misnomer, since the blast is not loud, but the effect on the nervous system is severe and instant. There was a bright flash, a muffled thump. More thumps. Glass breaking, something falling.

Kelly checked with his Thermospecs. "They're all down." He pulled out a small gun of his own, and loaded it with a glass ball. He sighted with the laserscope and fired the ball through the same window. They could hear it clatter against a wall, roll along the floor.

"Okay," Killy said. He pulled out a small mirrored disc from a small leather case.

"Portal," Kelly said. "Follow the bouncing ball."

There was a flash and a whoosh of some considerable violence. Killy and Kelly found themselves in the living room. Killy first thing picked up the glass ball at his feet and pocketed it.

"Portal recovered," he said.

The living room: a couch, some cushions, a pair of mattresses on the floor. A couple of tables loaded with scales, plastic baggies, packed weed. One guy was sitting on the couch when the sonic bomb hit, and there he fell, a bent heap, face tranquil with unconsciousness. Another one collapsed by the table in the kitchen, the broken glass around him from the coffee cup that fell with him.

"Fuck! We'll have to take Mendoza with us," Kelly said. "We don't have time for a chat!"

Killy found Jose "Crash" Mendoza in bed. He had fallen onto it, still clutching a smoking bong. The water stained the maroon bedsheet.

"Shit, he was smoking it," Kelly said, examining the dark residue in the bong.

He searched around for Moon Dust, looking through the thick cakes of weed, the bags of buds and leaves. Killy found a briefcase full of the stuff in the bedroom, Kelly a small leather pouch. Kelly time-jumped with it all back to the safehouse while Killy went back to the bedroom to check on Crash Mendoza. There was still time before these stoners would come to. Killy scanned all of them, checked their vital signs, and had just reached the bed when he noticed he could see the maroon sheet right through the guy. Crash was fading right before his eyes. He quickly scanned what was happening, getting footage of the irresistible moment when he put his hand right through the fading image of Crash. After a few seconds, just a ruffled sheet, an empty bed, the stink of bongwater.

"What happened?" It was Kelly, having returned from the safehouse. Killy showed him on the mini-screen. "Oh crap," Kelly said. And he rushed out to check on the others.

"I don't think they smoked it," Killy said, examining one of the bongs. "Only him."

"We've got to set up a trace and find him," Kelly said.

"Won't he eventually come back?"

Kelly was heading to the kitchen when he heard the sound.

Killy heard it too. It was a buzzing, familiar. Growing to a flaming sizzle.

"I don't think . . ." Kelly said as they gathered up their equipment, "that we'll have time to find out."

There was a bright flash. The far wall in the living room glowed as five figures rushed in. Time Control Enforcement Troopers stormed into the room. A number of loud cracks—flashes from particle guns already drawn. Killy fell sideways in mid-dive, folded up like a snail on a stick. More cracks, as Kelly flipped a table over. Troopers tumbled in all directions. Kelly crawled over to Killy, who was twitching, his body glowing strangely.

"Hold it right there!" one of the troopers yelled.

The firing stopped.

Kelly grabbed the twitching Killy in a tight embrace. "Consuelo," he said.

There was a brief flash. It was a quick blink. The two of them were gone.

"Fuck! They portal'd out!"

"How they do that?"

"McClaren! Set up a trace!"

The one called McClaren worked his tablet just as there came another flash. The troopers snapped to attention with a shout. McClaren, irritated to see the trace wasn't working, found himself staring into the face of the Regional Commander himself. It was a harsh, battered face, cheek once slashed by a meat cleaver, his glowering glass eye uncovered by his usual patch.

"Damnit," he said.

2.

Report to Commission C [SPECIAL]
FROM:

TIME CONTROL ENFORCEMENT [TCE]
REGIONAL COMMAND "D"
Colonel Johannes Belasco

As of date 201262-208==

Primary Report:
As Deputy Commander of all TCE Troopers in the fields of time, I wish to place a complaint with this board.

For the second time this month we have intercepted two commission agents on a "time disturbance" case. I have been briefed that these two agents, Randolph "Killy" Jones and Rick "Kelly" Santana, are working to correct a time imbalance, confirmed by Time Control "K" traces.

These two agents are operating in restricted jurisdictions. Their actions come up on random traces and of course our agents respond to all violations of the codes. There are no exceptions and TCE REGIONAL COMMAND "D" would never apologize for its agents doing their jobs.

I also request that information be given to this office regarding the nature and purpose of their actions in the time zones involved, so that ultimate effect can be certified by TIMELINE SURVEY. Only then should an investigation be launched, always under the auspices, and obeying the codes and jurisdictions of the TCE regional structure. "Killy and Kelly" are no such thing as private investigators. They are ex–TCE Troopers, thirteen years of service between them. And since washing out of the force, they've left a trail of time violations a mile long. Why don't these "agents" put in for clearances or apply for permits? Why don't they follow the rule of law with regard to time interference? Why do they feel they can somehow act independently of the TCE and its guidelines? And why has this commission enlisted the services of two suspicious characters instead of relying on the TCE which is already running its own investigation? They are a constant danger to that investigation. It is crucial that the commission share its files and all information pertaining to THE ZIEGLER FILE. If this is not done within the next twelve hours, I will sign a warrant for their arrest. These violations must be addressed, and jurisdictions respected.

I MUST ALSO POINT OUT that while Abraham Ziegler is missing, there is as yet no evidence that he is behind these recent events, or any reason to go outside code or sidestep TCE investigations which are more than well-equipped to handle the case. I hold the commission personally responsible for any setbacks resulting from this affair.

3.

The strange smell of burnt toast.

Jose "Crash" Mendoza woke up in a room. A dingy bulb, a tiny window. A room of brick walls and stone floor. His brain was sluggish, his limbs rusty and slow. He stood up and looked around. A couple of tires. An old *cajón*. A dirty old mirror, half covered in a dark cloak. Crash gave himself a good gander in the spotted glass, as if to make sure he was still . . . "he." His afro, wild and free, still in effect. His jeans jacket with the Puerto Rican flags on it, his street colors (and that included his prized Young Lords button and that Black Panthers patch). Made him feel good just from looking so wild, resistant, and *Afro-Rican*. It was Funkadelic, it was Hendrix. Reached for his afro-pick in his back pocket. (Yeah, reassuring feel of that plastic handle shaped like a small black fist.) Pulled it out to give his hair some flow action. But what's with this room? A slow brain, like when he smoked bad weed. Weed, weed . . . he remembered smoking weed, right? He looked around the room again. There was only that steel door. The way out.

Crash opened the door slow. He was in a small courtyard between buildings. There was a narrow alley through which he could make out street. A line of trash cans. He walked down the alley carefully, the sight of street growing bigger. Through the steel gate, there were people walking along. Cars rumbled by. A bullet-shaped bus picked up passengers across the street.

Stepping out through the gate, Crash recognized where he was. Prospect Avenue and 149th Street. The hardware store, boutique, dress factory, and pizzeria that used to make up the block were gone, replaced now by a . . . "superette," an auto parts store, and a restaurant of some Mexican persuasion. (Across the street was the same story. Whole buildings were gone, replaced by houses.) Walking over to Fox Street, he used to see rows of five-story tenements all the way to Avenue St. John. Only right now he couldn't. Fox Street didn't have buildings. It had funky two-story houses. Small green lawns. And that was as far as the eye could see.

It was Fox Street. But it wasn't Fox Street.

"What the fuck?" he said to a woman who paused to look at him. All of a sudden he noticed the people, many of them looking at him as he went by. Black people, and some people that could've been *Boricuas* . . . there were a lot of Mexicans. Their clothes looked big, jeans baggy, clumpy fat sneaks, and then the fucking Yankee caps, so many damn Yankee caps, so many backpacks, it was like a dress code. The cars! What happened to them? They looked swollen, puffy fat monsters, stubby and gray. There was a general sameness about them.

He crossed the street, checked street signs, shook his shaggy head. He was in the South Bronx. But what South Bronx was this? It was home, and not home. It was Southern Boulevard, but with different stores and shops. A cluster of teenagers by a stoop, all wearing the same kind of big jackets and leather baseball caps, reminded Crash of gangs. Savage Skulls? Nomads? No way remotely they would dress like that, but it made him wary. Whatever was going on, this wasn't his neighborhood anymore.

Back to the corner where the entrance to the subway still was, and there, a few feet away, was a newsstand, a funky metal booth with a guy inside selling newspapers. He picked up a copy and looked at the date: *WEDNESDAY, OCTOBER 23, 2012.*

Is this a joke? He checked the dates on the other papers and magazines. Words and pictures made him dizzy. Crash closed his eyes, caught his breath. Leaned against the cool metal of the kiosk's side. Opened his eyes. The mad whirl of buses and cars and people all around him. Not real. Real enough.

Little bits were coming back to him. They were moving the stuff, just to be on the safe side. And Pachuco would take some, and Wage and Daniel and Mike, and then they got into a fight because a few days before, Wage had been packing product for sale and came across the briefcase full of Moon Dust. He figured it was product and that's how some of it ended up out on the street.

The Moon Dust! The special glittery weed! Crash had started smoking it! He remembered being in his bedroom, smoking the Moon Dust . . . and then, FLASH . . . he started walking up 149th Street. Where was Daniela's Hair Salon, and the *cuchifritería* that used to smell up the block with its fried pork rinds in the window under a lightbulb? PS 25 was still there, but he didn't recognize anything on the way to St. Mary's Park. Going there unlocked a whole mess of memories. What kind of stuff was this, this Moon

Dust, that made his real life seem like murky images of a remembered dream?

Up the big hill. The spot was still there, the stone steps leading down to the street and the projects, all of it coming to him in driblets. Sure, he had been busted before. Seven ounces was the safe side, and he and his boys did a wild dance with the stuff. It was skill. It was the fucken Puerto Rican *samba*. And he didn't care what anybody said about it, these *lambe-ojo hijo de putas*—what Jose "Crash" Mendoza was doing was resistance. Was the righteous war. Was a fucken crusade against an unfair, oppressive, and racist system. Being against it was as Puerto Rican as . . . *mofongo*, damnit. It was an act of survival to sell weed in the devil's city. He and his boys were a tight band of resistance! Sitting around the pad on St. Anne's. Hitting Honey Bear bongs and tripping on black-light posters of black Amazonian chicks while blaring the Funkadelic.

This one day they had cleared the bushes twice already and Crash had just sent Mike back to pick up some more product. No cops in sight so they were feeling pretty loose, just smoking cigarettes and talking with some dudes over by the benches. There was this white hippie dude there, popped out of nowhere. Young, long-haired, patched-up jeans. Just when they were clear that they were all on the same resistance wavelength, the guy got down to business.

"I have an offer to make you, bro," he said. "I represent a select collective of heads who have cultivated a rare and precious weed."

Now Crash was open to this. He had heard about honkies coming up here to make drug deals. Sometimes they wanted to buy. Sometimes they were offering a new connection as a way to establish a presence in the Bronx, like what happened to Jelly Boy and his crew when they started getting weed from the Jamaicans.

The hippie started by talking about some pothead collective, but ended up going on about "The Doctor" and how he was rich and infiltrating the system from underneath and he was making Crash an amazing deal where Crash would get double the product and make double the bread. And as a sample, the hippie produced a small leather bag . . . and a briefcase . . .

Crash unzipped the small leather bag. There, wrapped in plastic, were some of the sweetest buds he had seen in a while. Bright green, looked fresh and hydroponic, but there was something else, something glittery. At first he thought it was the plastic, but no. There was a silvery, sparkly dust on the stuff.

"Hey, wild! What kinda psychedelic shit is that! Whass this shit on it, man?"

"It's the future. Let's just call it *super hydro*. Normal weed, you gotta smoke more to get the same high. Moon Dust builds up in your system. It has a trigger effect, like acid flashback. Except," the hippie started to laugh, "it's no flashback. It's a flash forward. It accumulates, it goes farther. Until finally you cross a barrier. You time travel, bro." The hippie's eyes were wild and feverish. "You try the stuff. There's a card in the bag. Call the number. The Doctor is always reachable," the hippie laughed, "even when you're smoked. No matter what time it is."

Words. Slapping of hands. Then the hippie walked off into the bushes, and vanished.

Thirty-eight years later, the place was virtually the same, even the projects were still up. But there were no dealers, no action. There was no group of dudes hanging out on the benches, playing bongos and congas. It was quiet and lonely. A Mexican kid and his father kicked a soccer ball around. People strolling. Crash sat on the hill and looked down on the green stillness. This wasn't from his imagination. None of it was. It was the Moon Dust.

The Doctor is always reachable. That cackly hippie laugh. *No matter what time it is.*

Crash stood up, reaching for his wallet. *FUTURE TECHNOLOGIES INC.*, the card read. He walked off the hill and headed down 149th Street, toward Third Avenue. He kept looking for a pay phone, but he didn't see any, all the way to Third Avenue. A busy hub as always; Crash tried to take in the changes. Hearns, the big department store, was gone, giving way to a ton of small stores, including phone shops . . . phones, those little things are phones!! But they're so small . . . Finally found a pay phone there by the subway entrance. He popped in some quarters and punched the number out on the keypad. There was a series of clicks. A strange buzzing sound. A slow set of rings. Someone picked up.

"Future," a woman's voice said.

Crash was breathless for a moment. "The Doctor," he said. "I want to speak to Dr. Robert."

"What portal are you?" she asked.

"Portal? I don't know."

"What was your method of transit?"

Crash thought a moment, and grinned like he was getting it. "Moon Dust," he said.

"Oh, right, sorry! Hold on." There was a click. Crash waited, feeling woozy. He was making a phone call while tripping.

"Hello, this is Dr. Robert." The voice was old and gentle, the kind of voice Crash had heard in an Uncle Ben's Converted Rice commercial. "And how do you feel right now, Mr. Mendoza?"

"You know me?"

"But of course. You're the only person in time that has this number. You've gone thirty-eight years into the future. Moon Dust is a cheap, simple way of getting people into the time stream. To violate it, corrupt it. Temporary, but effective as a means of infiltration."

"I don't understand," Crash said, his head starting to spin.

"Time travel is strictly regulated and controlled. It's against the law for people to travel through time. They fear that people going back in time can find a way to put their system out of business. Create a resistance. Fight the system."

"I'm all for that," Crash said. "But—"

"There's so much more to tell you, but right now you have to keep moving."

"What?"

"Phoning through time is traceable. Take the subway to Union Square. Whatever you do, don't get arrested. I'll send someone to you to insure you fade."

"Arrested? Insure I fade? What? Hello?" There was a clicking, then, *"Please deposit twenty-five cents for the next five minutes or your call will be interrupted."*

"Twenty-five cents?? Hello?"

The line went dead.

The subway station looked mostly the same. Crash always had tokens on him but there was no coin slot. He watched people going in through the turnstile. They were swiping a card. Over by the wall, he saw a lady stick dollar bills into a machine. (At least the dollar bills were the same.) She was touching the screen. Huh!? After she left, he checked it out, even touching the screen, but decided to take his chances with the token-booth clerk. The white-haired black man was hardly visible through the thick glass. Crash got behind someone and watched the guy slip a five-dollar bill in the slot. Five bucks!? What the fuck!? Crash followed suit. The clerk gave him a MetroCard. Took him awhile to swipe it right, but then he was through the turnstile and waiting on the platform for a train whose glimmery lights were already visible in the tunnel distance. The TV screens were new and he could see himself leaning over the platform to look. A train passing on the uptown side. Silver bullets on wheels, not the blue-grays from 1973. And these made a funny howling sound, all nervous jittery.

The roar and blast of subway train pulling into station. The inside of the train was brighter but felt more cluttered. Crash stared wide-eyed at the moving ads, the screens flashing messages. A solitary marker scrawl on the wall of no decipherable message, seemed like the last graffiti in the world.

He sat by the doors. The people in the car were not even looking at each other. Everybody was busy with something. The lady across from him was typing on her phone, her pretty fingers moving nimbly across the small screen. Many people wearing earphones. A girl across the way tapping the screen of a tablet. Everybody was busy. There was not one person staring into space, falling asleep, or reading a book. At least there was one guy at the end there, reading a newspaper. The mechanical voice on the PA: "*Backpacks and other personal belongings are subject to random search.*" The guy reading the newspaper got up and left the newspaper. Crash slid over and scooped it up. It was a copy of the *Village Voice*. The poster on the wall opposite showed a package beside a subway bench. Is that right, so America has a black president? *Beware of Suspicious Packages*. (A strange thrill.)

"I'm reading a paper from the future," he said, needing to hear the words. The black girl across from him was looking right at him, but she didn't react. Her eyes were glazed, head bopping to earphones. He flipped through the newspaper again.

"America's first black president is running for reelection." The Twin Towers in flames. "Since 9/11, America has been fighting the war on terrorism." American soldiers in Afghanistan. "Protests call for an end to 'Stop and Frisk.'" Who's Kim Kardashian? "Of the six hundred thousand New Yorkers stopped and frisked last year, only nine percent were white." American soldiers in Iraq. *If You See Something, Say Something*. What kinda shit is this? "The latest move from the city that's set trends by banning smoking in bars and trans fats in foods involves banning sugary drinks sold at restaurants, fast-food chains, theaters, delis, office cafeterias, and other places that fall under the New York City Board of Health's regulation, by March 2013."

Crash started to feel weird. He shut the paper, looking up at an ad that showed a Mexican family. *Learn English.* Oh shit. The train rocked and whined. People were giving him weird looks. Something was strangely oppressive. He got off the train at Union Square, went up the stairs to the main concourse, and spotted a group of people dressed all funky crazy. One was a colorful jester, a black kid with bells on his hat that jingled. There was a jockey, a princess, and there was this pretty blonde in an Alice in Wonderland dress that walked right up to him.

"Well, well. What kept you?" Her eyes were green, her blond hair raining down in loopy curls. She looked somehow familiar to him. He wondered if it was because she had a vague resemblance to Susan Sarandon.

"Are you . . . ?" Crash couldn't even say.

"Of course," she answered, laughing, turning, and pulling someone over. "And here's the Doctor!"

A young guy in a doctor's suit, white and clean. Obviously not the old Dr. Robert! He pressed his stethoscope to Crash's chest, took a listen.

"Yes," he said, "definitely alive."

"I love your hair," the Princess said, almost touching it.

"Hey, man," the Jester said, his bells ringing, "you a real sight. "You lucky they din't stop you, lookin' like that."

"What does that mean?"

"New York cops got the hots for people of color," the Jester said.

"What the hell's *people of color?*"

"Thass you, dog."

"Dog?" Crash frowned. "Hey, who the fuck are you people? Why are you dressed up like that?"

"We're going to a party," Alice said. She hooked her arm with his. "And we're bringing you. It's a costume thing, see? Jockey, Doctor, I'm the Alice, see? You're '70s Dude. And we even have a Jester and a Princess."

Crash looked from one to the other.

"Are you people on something?"

They laughed, a drunken swimmy laugh, a rollicking happy vibe that irritated him.

"We kinda make you less conspicuous, don't we?" Alice winked. "Come."

They started walking, the Jester's bells ringing, the Jockey twirling a walking stick, the Princess swinging her star on a wand. "Manhattan ain't nothing anymore but a mall for NYU students," Alice said. "The action's in Brooklyn."

L train. Sips from a canteen of rum and cola.

"Do you have a portal?" the Doctor asked. A young white guy, the boy next door.

"I don't even know what that is," Crash said.

Alice held a round mirrored disc in front of his face. It was the size of a coaster. Just a little round mirror.

"This is a portal," Alice said. "Moon Dust? It's made from this." Alice was looking at Crash and just smiling, a weird spirit thing. Crash was feeling it. Like the almost-touch of acid. "Moon Dust is just one of many ways the Doctor has . . . invented . . . to introduce people to the resistance."

"But why?"

"You see the way things are now. They're going to get worse."

"But there's a black president!"

Their laughter drowned out the roar of the train pulling into Bedford. The station was crammed with young people. There were more white people there than he had ever seen in one place, except for maybe that Ten Years After concert he went to at Randall's Island . . . that bevy of girl asses in skimpy shorts going up the stairs . . . On the street, a throbbing energy of lights, bars, cars, girls in tight pants and short skirts showing off long nylon legs . . . Crash was swimming a little from the rum maybe.

Bar after bar along the street, music blaring through open windows, and this one especially, blaring Hendrix.

"Now you're talkin'," he said.

Alice nodded to the others and they all went into the bar where Hendrix was singing about crosstown traffic. Alice bought Crash a beer. The Princess was dancing in a corner with the Doctor. The Jockey was poring over the pizza menu with the Jester.

Alice clinked beers with him, words coming in snippets and bits. Crash had too many questions. "I can't answer all that." But her eyes. The way she looked at him. Somehow, the promise of an eternal fuck. The music went from Hendrix to Cream, from Cream to the Rolling Stones. How was it Santana all of a sudden, doing "Samba Pa Ti"? The lilting congas and that crooning guitar. Pressing close, slow moving, and she was feeling fine against him. When the song ended, her hands slid up his shoulders and around his neck. Her swimmy eyes closed beautifully slow. She kissed him. It was a sloppy, sudden kiss, but not rushed. It had sincerity.

"I don't even know your name," he said.

"There are things I'm supposed to tell you this time." She had both his hands. "My name isn't one of them."

"This time?"

"Yeah." She was squeezing his hands. "The Doctor looks for people, special people. Like you, Jose."

"Oh yeah? And what makes me so special?"

"You're Puerto Rican," she said.

"Look, man, I know how it feels to be picked on because I'm Puerto Rican, or picked OUT because I'm Puerto Rican, but this being *chosen* thing . . ."

"You don't understand. You're Puerto Rican," she said, "from a time when there were Puerto Ricans."

"What does that fucking mean, man? You tellin' me there ain't no Puerto Ricans where you come from?"

She held his hands, didn't say anything. Her face glowed with something grown-up and painful.

"Hey, you're scaring me . . ."

"I wish I could promise you a future, but I can't." Her eyes glistened wetly.

"But what happened to the Puerto Ricans?"

"Every person we bring in has a chance to change everything for the better. It might be your destiny. To change destiny."

Crash was feeling a weird heat burning his face.

"Are you saying something bad is gonna happen to my people?"

"I'm not supposed to." Why were her eyes wet? "You may fade soon, so . . ." Pretty eyes, quick blinking.

"What does that mean?"

She laughed, then spotted something over his shoulder.

"Fuck," she said, "fuck fuck fuck! Adrian!" she yelled over the music to the Doctor. "*Arriverderci, Roma!*"

"What's going on?" Crash asked, turning to look.

She was gripping him frantic. "It's the fuzz, jack!"

Crash glanced around, frantic. He wished the music would stop. The Jockey, the Princess, and the Doctor were nowhere in sight. When he turned again it seemed the Jester had vanished with a clink of bells.

Alice touched his face, her eyes determined and strange.

"I'll find you again," she said. A peck on the lips. Then she shoved him. He fell against an empty table, chair crashing to floor, people scurrying. He didn't see where she went. Someone grabbed his arm as he was getting up.

"Well, well," a voice said. "If it isn't 1973."

It was a tall thin man holding his arm, a man peculiarly dressed in a bowler hat and pinstripe suit.

"Who the fuck are you?" Crash shook his arm loose.

"They portal'd out," explained another one, who was larger but dressed the same. Partners.

"Time cops?" Crash said it like he was spitting out soap. "Are you serious?"

"You should be grateful we're *not* time cops," Killy said, "because you don't want to know what they do to accidental time trippers like you. No, you don't."

"Get your hands off me," Crash snapped, giving Killy a shove that sent him reeling backward. Then he felt a burning heat strike him like a blow.

4.

FLASH . . . to wake up heavy with a dream he couldn't remember, just bits of image and face . . . He woke up, rethinking it over and over as he sat in his bed . . . Crash felt like he couldn't breathe. He opened the window, all the way up with a jarring noise that blurred the street below for a moment. It was Fox Street, looking east toward Prospect Avenue. It was rows of rows of grungy tenements, of people in the windows and kids on fire escapes and people on stoops. And the crack of a stickball bat and the rush and squeak of sneaks on asphalt. And that sound, it was in the air. Not just laughter and pots and pans . . . it was trombones it was timbales it was Puerto Rican salsa music. It was Héctor Lavoe singing and every Puerto Rican household saying, "Oh yes, come on in." The sound was everywhere, in the walls and upstairs and out in the alley. Crash couldn't say why his eyes filled with tears. Something here, and not forever.

Walking out into the living room, the usual picture. Mike was sprawled on the couch, sucking on a Honey Bear and watching the TV. Pachuco was playing the O'Jays on the stereo. Wage was sitting out on the fire escape doing his "post" routine. Crash went over to the corner, where there were some garbage bags on a table. He checked through them, the baggies of buds, packed product, ready to move.

"Hey," Daniel said. He had just come out of the kitchen. "You sure were out for a long time."

"Some kind of dream," he said. "I can't remember, but . . ."

Crash was trying to process all the bits of image and picture and face, sparks from a twitching live wire. The general commotion of the guys collecting their stuff and heading out, splitting up and meeting up, all prearranged and flawlessly perfected, little sidesteps to keep the man guessing. Crash fell into the routine and it was good, doing something calmed the jittery confusion in his head. And then there was a flow, and he hardly noticed time going by at all. They had cleared the bushes twice already and Crash had just sent Mike back to pick up some more product. No cops in sight so they were feeling pretty loose, just smoking cigarettes and talking with some dudes over by the benches, when this little white girl appeared out of nowhere. She was young, blond, a sort of hippie in flared, patched-up jeans. She didn't seem uptight about being in the ghetto, and the guys were all lighting on her. Pachuco even cranked his portable cassette player to increase the vibe and maybe get her to dance, but slim hips only had eyes for Crash. The way she looked at him. Somehow, the promise of an eternal fuck. The music went from Hendrix to Cream, from Cream to the Rolling Stones, as Pachuco searched the tape for the proper soundtrack for the white girl. How was it Santana all of a sudden, doing "Samba Pa Ti"? The lilting congas and that crooning guitar. Her tongue twirling redly around that Charms Blow Pop.

"I have an offer to make you," she said, opening her purse.

A beaded thing. Crash peeked inside. Saw the weed all glittery sparkling.

Now Crash was open to this . . .

Seth Kushner

Dean Haspiel is an Emmy Award winner and Eisner Award nominee. He created *BILLY DOGMA*, illustrated for HBO's *Bored to Death*, received a residency at Yaddo, and was a master artist at the Atlantic Center for the Arts. Haspiel has written and drawn many superhero and semi-autobiographical comix, including collaborations with Harvey Pekar, Jonathan Ames, Inverna Lockpez, and Jonathan Lethem. He also curates and creates for TripCity.net.

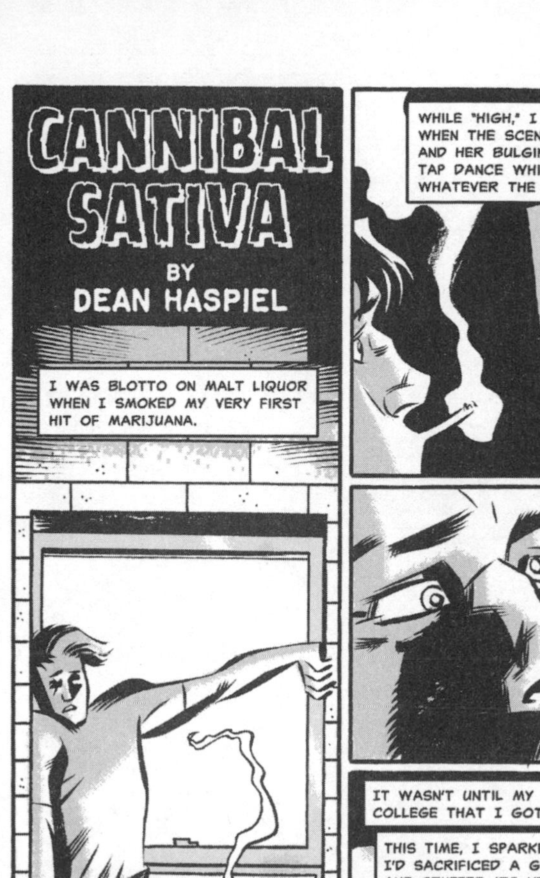
CANNIBAL SATIVA
BY DEAN HASPIEL
I WAS BLOTTO ON MALT LIQUOR WHEN I SMOKED MY VERY FIRST HIT OF MARIJUANA.

WHILE "HIGH," I WATCHED DAVID LYNCH'S ERASERHEAD WHEN THE SCENE WITH THE CREEPY RADIATOR LADY AND HER BULGING CHEEKS CAME ON, DOING HER SLOW TAP DANCE WHILE DODGING FALLING ABORTIONS OR WHATEVER THE HELL THOSE DEMONIC DROPPINGS WERE!

I WENT BANANAS AND NEARLY JUMPED SEVEN STORIES OUT OF MY UPPER WEST SIDE APARTMENT WINDOW.

IT WASN'T UNTIL MY FRESHMEN YEAR OF COLLEGE THAT I GOT STONED AGAIN.
THIS TIME, I SPARKED A GNARLY RUMOR THAT I'D SACRIFICED A GOAT FROM A NEARBY FARM AND STUFFED ITS HEAD IN MY REFRIGERATOR.

I COERCED SEVERAL STUDENTS TO VIEW MY "SACRIFICE" AND LET ONE CHUMP IN AT A TIME LIKE AT THOSE CIRCUS FREAK ACTS.

MOST OF THE LIGHTS IN MY ROOM WERE CUT OFF AND I'D BEND DOWN IN THE DARK, HOLD MY NOSE, OPEN THE FRIDGE DOOR, WAVE FAKE STENCH WITH MY FREE HAND, GAG FROM THE PHANTOM ROTTEN MEAT, LET THEM THINK THEY SAW THE GOAT HEAD FOR A SPLIT SECOND, AND SLAM THE FRIDGE DOOR SHUT.
MY THESPIAN SKILLS WERE OSCAR AWARD WORTHY BECAUSE THEY WOULD GET NAUSEOUS AND RUN AWAY, SPREADING CAMPUS RUMORS ABOUT MY IMPROMPTU DORM ROOM CULT.
WHO KNEW THE SMELL OF CHARCOAL-FILTERED MALT LIQUOR, A BALLED UP, DIRTY PILLOW CASE, AND THE POWER OF SUGGESTION WOULD MAKE FOR SUCH A CONVINCING COMBO?
A WEEK LATER, THE DEAN OF DISCIPLINE ASKED TO TALK WITH ME AND I HAD SOME EXPLAINING TO DO.
SOCIETY
WHEN I GOT LOOSELY ACCLIMATED TO MARIJUANA, I REALIZED IT JUST PUT ME TO SLEEP AND I WAS MORE INTERESTED IN CLIMBING THE WALLS.
I GAVE UP THE GANJA.
THE END

"I liked you too, Martin," I had said. This was perfectly true. I did like him. I just didn't like his head.

Eventually, I made Alexander Vinokourov get off my lap so I could stand up. I opened the drawer where I keep my socks and underwear. I pulled out the powder-blue plastic wallet with *Wyoming* emblazoned on its side.

There'd been a time when I thought Alexander Vinokourov and I might move to Wyoming. I've had ideas about moving to many places and have in fact moved to most of them. Lately, though, I just keep drifting around a hundred-mile radius of upstate New York. It's pretty here and the people aren't all morons. My rent is cheap and I can get by doing odd jobs.

I put the blue plastic wallet in the back pocket of my jeans, attached Vino's leash to his collar, and out we went.

It was hot outside and, even though it was close to dusk, the sun was a burning gold coin.

Vino and I walked up to the top of State Street where crumbling buildings rested their crooked frames against newly renovated ones.

The guy with hooks for arms was sitting on his porch and called out: "Beautiful dog!"

I said, "Thank you," like I had made Alexander Vinokourov myself.

We reached the periphery of the cemetery, where the sign reads, *Cemetery closed during hours of darkness.*

We walked in through the oldest section, where half the tombstones have toppled and time has rubbed off the dead people's names. We crossed to the far side, past the war veteran's area where there'd been a big kerfuffle when vandals had started stealing all the flags off the graves. Video surveillance had been set up to catch the perpetrators in the act and had caught . . . woodchucks. They were stealing the flags and taking them to their woodchuck holes.

zombie hookers of hudson
by maggie estep

One morning, his head looked too small and I asked him to move out.

Why? He stared at me.

"It's just not working," I said. I didn't mention that his head suddenly appeared small. You can't say that to someone. It's not right. "I'm not happy," I said.

Martin's eyes drooped and then he shrugged.

He'd only been living with me three weeks.

He packed up his stuff and, just like that, he was gone.

We'd started as strangers, we were ending that way.

Then it was just me and Alexander Vinokourov, my one-eared pit bull, Vino to his friends.

I sat on the floor with Alexander Vinokourov in my lap, his head wedged under my arm. His head is too large for his body, but I like that. Imperfections in dogs are beautiful; in humans they're a fault line that you want to put a jackhammer in.

I sat like that, numb and quiet, for about thirty minutes. I was like a cow needing to be squeezed for reassurance before going into one of the *humane* slaughter chutes designed by the admirable Temple Grandin. Vino was my sixty-eight-pound squeezing machine. Except I wasn't heading to slaughter. At least not that I was aware of.

I stared at the empty drawers where Martin's stuff had been. I thought about his last words to me.

"I really liked you, Zoey."

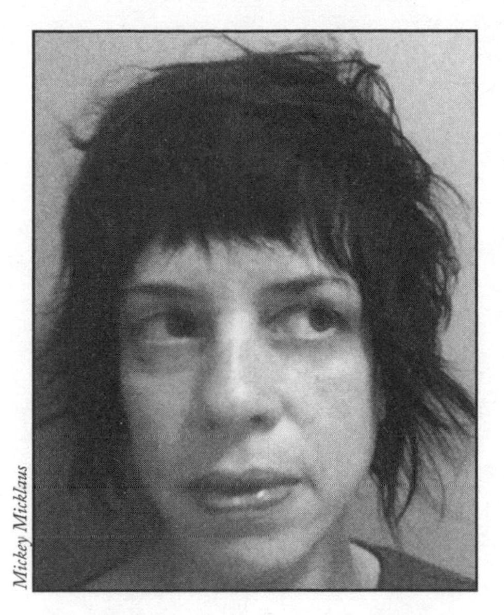

Mickey Micklaus

Maggie Estep is the author of seven books. Her work has been translated into four languages, optioned for film, and frequently stolen from libraries. She lives in Hudson, New York.

They liked the taste of the cured wood the flags were attached to.

Vino and I walked to our favorite spot, a wooded, quiet area lying between the cemetery and the new artificial sweetener factory, the building which had caused nearly as big a kerfuffle as the flag-stealing woodchucks.

But something was wrong. An excavator had been here and dug up a huge swath of earth, maybe half an acre, and there was now a gaping maw where Vino's favorite grassy knoll had been.

We went to stand at the edge of this big mouth in the earth. I saw pieces of broken-up wooden boxes strewn around in the dirt below.

I didn't like it. Didn't like the artificial sweetener factory, didn't like that Vino's favorite grassy knoll had been dug up for reasons I wasn't sure about—but probably had to do with the sweetener factory.

I didn't like much of anything that day.

I took the Wyoming wallet out of my back pocket, sat at the edge of the hole in the ground, dangled my legs over, and, as Vino flopped down and started panting, I took my small stash of weed out of the wallet and rolled a joint. This was excellent weed. Had a tense, earthy smell, almost exactly like the big dirt hole I was staring at.

I lit the joint then coughed. Alexander Vinokourov's head swiveled toward me, making sure I wasn't dying. I'm never sure if his concern for my well being is entirely altruistic. If I die, he'll have to go back to scavenging from garbage cans and escaping thugs trying to trap him and turn him into a fighting dog.

I took another hit and coughed again, but this time Vino merely flicked his ear, listening for sounds of serious distress before bothering to turn his entire head.

My own head was taking a beating from the inside out, the weed making me feel like I'd had an involuntary hemispherectomy, the two sides of my brain operating independently of each other which, I was pretty sure, would lead to something unusual and very possibly unpleasant.

Then, just as the letters of the word *unpleasant* drifted through my mind, something reached up from the pit in the earth and grabbed my ankle.

I screamed.

Alexander Vinokourov was next to me in an instant and we both looked down to see a horrible mud-covered woman with her hands around my ankle.

My heart hammered. Vino was trembling. Adrenalin coursed through me, but it was paralyzing rather than giving me superhuman strength. I stared at this creature with her fingers digging into the flesh of my ankle. I tried to shake my leg free before this freak pulled my ankle out of its socket.

I screamed for help but there wasn't anyone to hear me.

Then, suddenly, the woman made a sound, like a cat coughing up a large hairball, and let go of my ankle.

I turned around and ran, slowing down only when I was about a hundred yards away. I looked back, expecting to find the muddy woman coming after me. She was not.

I stood there, my body flooded with fear chemicals, my mind burning with curiosity. Then I heard an unmistakable cry for help. The voice was reedy, small, pathetic.

"Please. Help," she repeated.

I guess I was more stoned than I realized. I walked back over to the edge of that maw in the earth and peered down. The woman had dirt caked in her hair and was wearing what may have once been a dress but now looked like the Shroud of Turin.

Her eyes met mine. She looked very sad.

"Who are you?" I asked.

She didn't answer right away and she was staring at something, maybe Vino, maybe something past me.

"May I have some, please?" she asked.

"Have some what?"

"Some tea," she said, motioning toward the sky.

I looked up at the sky too. It was just past dusk, almost all dark up there, a lemon slice of moon starting to show itself.

"Tea?" I said looking back down at her.

"Tea," the woman repeated, pointing, it seemed, at my hand.

I looked at my hand too. The joint. I was holding the half-smoked joint. I had some dim memory of pot being called *tea*. Like in the 1950s.

"You want a hit of *this?*"

The muddy woman nodded.

Was this really happening? I relit the joint and passed it to her, reaching down just far enough so she could take it but couldn't pull on any of my body parts.

She smiled. She had dirt between her teeth.

She took an enormous hit. She didn't cough, but her blue eyes bulged. Eventually, she tried passing it back up to me but I declined. She might be contagious.

"Could you help me get out of here?" she asked, then.

She had a strange way of speaking, not an accent really, but a lilt. She was reaching up toward me like a little kid wanting to be lifted up onto a parent's shoulders. I actually felt sorry for her.

I reached down and took the woman's dirty wrists into my hands and pulled.

One of my odd jobs is as a dog handler at the local animal shelter. I routinely lift very large dogs up onto examination tables. This woman didn't weigh much more than Henry, the mastiff who was endlessly scraping himself up.

She clambered up, her bare feet finding purchase in the wall of earth. Then, exhausted from this effort, she fell belly-first in the grass. She looked dead. Alexander Vinokourov went over to sniff the air around her. I was about to nudge her with my foot when she rolled over and sat up.

"Are you all right?" I asked, squinting at her.

There was mud caked in her eyelashes.

"No," she said simply. Again, she tried passing the joint back to me.

I looked all around. The woman was, after all, at least half-naked and totally covered in mud and we were just a few feet away from Newman Road, the street that skirts one side of the cemetery and leads to the dump. Some guy in a pickup truck was bound to drive by at any moment, get turned on at the sight of my muddy friend, and come running over.

There was no one around though. The road was quiet and my lust for the joint outweighed any concern about contagion. I took another hit and felt a little calmer.

"Do you want me to walk you over to the hospital?" I asked. If I took her to the cops, they'd eventually pack her off to the psych ward anyway. It would be kinder to just take her there directly.

"But I'm not ill, I'm dead. Or was dead." She said it with a straight face.

"Ah."

"You don't believe me. But it's true. I was dead. Buried. Then, two days ago, I woke. There were sounds. Earth-moving machines. Digging us up, digging up the pine boxes that we were buried in. In 1924."

I sighed. I looked at my dog. My dog looked at me. "I'm sorry. I can walk you to the hospital if you'd like, but that's all I can do."

"Noooo," she shook her head. Her muddy hair moved.

"Then I can't help you." I turned my back, even as she called out to me.

"My name is Annabelle," she said, trying to humanize herself, imprint herself on me.

I ignored her, though I could feel her eyes on my back as I retreated.

I got home, took Vino's leash off, then immediately smoked another joint. I usually don't smoke at home for fear of attracting neighbors wanting to bum weed off me. But after you've had an encounter with a woman who claims to be dead, it is sometimes necessary to smoke at home.

I was hungry. I walked into the kitchen with its bright yellow linoleum tiles, relentlessly cheerful, even at night. I opened the fridge. There was meat for Vino, but not much for me. A shrunken head of lettuce. A pear. A jar of almond butter. Maybe I'd walk over to the tortilla truck on Warren Street.

I went into the bathroom and looked at myself in the full-length mirror. My black T-shirt and jeans were covered in mud and dog hair. My own hair, well past my shoulders, was in nests. I leaned over the big porcelain sink and threw water on my face. I ran my fingers through my hair. I put on lip gloss.

I was looking at myself in the mirror when suddenly Annabelle appeared there, standing right behind me.

I screamed, reached for the nearest object, and pointed it at her. It was a hairbrush.

"How did you get in here?" I shoved the hairbrush, bristles-first, into Annabelle's stomach.

"Ouch!" She looked like I'd hurt her feelings more than her physical vessel. You left me there, left all of us there," she said. Her eyebrows moved like muddy caterpillars as she motioned beyond the bathroom.

I craned my neck and saw two more muddy women behind her. I screamed again.

Vino barked.

"Get the fuck out of my house!" I attacked Annabelle with my hairbrush, backing her against the sink.

"Shhh, please, hush," Annabelle said.

"I will not hush. You hush. And get out of my house."

She didn't move and the other two just stood there too, staring.

I felt nauseous. "What are you doing here?" I asked Annabelle. "You followed me?" I was having trouble breathing.

"We need help," Annabelle said. "We're hungry. Me and Birdie and Sophia." She motioned at her compatriots. Birdie was tall and skinny, Sophia short and curvy. They were both covered in mud just like Annabelle. How they had walked through downtown Hudson without getting arrested or raped, I wasn't sure. It's a laissez-faire town, but not that laissez.

"And what, I look like a fucking soup kitchen?"

"Please help us." This entreaty came from Sophia, the shortest of the women.

"Please get out of my house."

Vino barked again but it's not as if he did anything useful, like look menacing for example.

Now, Birdie, the tall one, started talking in an excited high voice telling me that all three of them had been murdered some ninety years earlier by a man named Giacomo.

"Giacomo?" I said numbly.

"He was our pimp," explained Sophia, putting a fist on her hip and tilting her chin.

"You're *hookers*?"

"Whores, yes," Annabelle nodded. "And don't go putting on airs, it's not like you're some sort of aristocrat, Zoey."

"No. It's not like that at all." I didn't remember telling her my name. "So you were hookers and your pimp named Giacomo killed you ninety years ago," I said. "Why did he do that?"

"We stole money from him," Birdie said. "And then he poisoned us."

"It was a very painful death," Sophia said.

"Can you excuse me a minute, please?" I said. "I need to pee."

I pushed Annabelle out of the bathroom and closed the door, keeping my dog with me so they didn't try doing weird dead-person stuff to him.

I took several deep breaths.

I had my phone in my pocket. Could I call Martin? Ask him to come back? Tell him that there were three zombie hookers in my house? Probably not.

I thought of calling my best friend, Janie, but she was two hours away, in Manhattan, and would probably be completely useless in this situation. Almost anyone would be. I peered through the bathroom door keyhole. They were still standing there. Like zombies. Staring at the bathroom door, willing me to come back out.

"We're really hungry!" Sophia called out.

I wondered if they could see through doors.

I didn't know what to do, so I fed them.

They ate ice cream, smoked all the pot in my Wyoming wallet, then passed out on my sleeper sofa.

As they slept, I sat in my armchair and watched them. I was fascinated, horrified.

I got up and tiptoed closer to get a better look. Birdie, bony and elegant with a sharp nose and cheekbones like knives, was lying on her back with her mouth open. Sophia, round and soft, was curled onto her side. Annabelle, the exotic, dark-haired one, lay flat on her stomach. They looked almost lovely, innocent.

I got my laptop and went back to the chair, Googled *zombies*. This yielded what you'd expect. The tongue-in-cheek Zombie Apocalypse Preparedness tips issued by the Center for Disease Control. Definitions of zombies as moaning, brain-eating monsters, spawned to popularity by George Romero. Viral ghouls that bore little resemblance to the sweetly slumbering dead hookers on my sofa.

I sent an e-mail to an acquaintance, Doon, a neuroscientist with an interest in things that science can't easily explain.

I pointed my phone at the zombies, snapped a photo, and sent it with the e-mail. I don't KNOW Doon very well. He's the son of an Alzheimer's patient I used to care for as one of my odd jobs. He would probably completely ignore my e-mail. Or maybe refer me to a mental health professional.

I wondered if my zombies were contagious. I wondered if there were more of them. If maybe dozens of dead denizens had been reanimated when the earth-moving machine had dug up that swath of land at the cemetery's edge. Then I went to sleep.

When I woke, I had forgotten about the dead hookers. Vino was at the foot of the bed and wagged his tail when he saw I was awake. I scratched him behind the ear. He licked my nose. I was heading into the kitchen when I remembered. Mostly because there they were, on my sleeper sofa.

Fuck.

As they started to stir I noticed they didn't look so good. All three seemed sort of desiccated, and as Birdie unfurled herself from the sleeper sofa, I could swear I heard her bones creaking.

"I don't feel well," she said.

"I don't either," Annabelle chimed in, propping herself up on one elbow.

"I have to get coffee."

I walked into the kitchen and flipped the switch on the coffee maker. I can't deal with anything before coffee. Certainly not zombies.

Alexander Vinokourov was dancing in anticipation of breakfast when Birdie came hobbling into the kitchen. She looked over my shoulder when I opened the fridge to get the plastic container of Performance Dog raw meat.

"I like meat," Birdie said.

"This is for the dog," I replied. "It has tripe and trachea. It's not for humans."

"I don't care," Birdie insisted.

I sighed. I filled Vino's bowl and put it on the floor. Then I took a plate from the cupboard, spooned out some meat, and handed it to Birdie.

"Let me get you a fork," I said, but the word *fork* wasn't even out of my mouth before she'd started using her fingers to scoop the bloody flesh into her mouth. She ate every last scrap, then, holding the plate to her face, licked it clean.

"Do you have any more tea?" Sophia had wandered into the kitchen now. She was wearing my fuzzy slippers and a dingy white T-shirt. She was naked from the waist down.

"No, I don't," I said. "You guys smoked all my pot. And ate all my ice cream," I added, a little resentfully.

Birdie and Sophia both looked at me like I had broken some law of basic decency by bemoaning their consumption of petty, replaceable things like weed and a one-gallon tub of butter pecan ice cream.

"We need tea," Sophia said.

"I don't have any more." *You weed-hogging dead hooker houseguest from hell,* I thought. "And it's illegal."

"It makes us feel better," Sophia said.

"It does," Birdie concurred.

"It makes lots of people feel better," I said. "But I don't have any more. You smoked my entire stash. If you want more weed, you'll have to go turn some tricks or something."

"What?" Annabelle joined in, her delicate face pinched.

I was pretty sure I was going to have a nervous breakdown.

Instead, I decided to walk my dog, leaving the zombies in my apartment. Putting on my huge sunglasses so the world couldn't see me.

Alexander Vinokourov and I had been walking for a while and were making our way up Warren Street, the main drag, when his ear shot straight up in the air and he started pulling on the leash.

He led me right over to the front of the drugstore where I saw none other than Sophia, leaning on a parking meter, smoking a cigarette. She was batting her eyelashes at a very large man who was grinning, showing off a gold-tooth grill. She was dressed in my clothes. A pair of jeans that clung to her, a button-down white shirt kittenishly knotted above her belly button, and, incongruously, my black combat boots that were clearly too big and made her look like a child.

Vino went right up to Sophia and licked her hand. As Sophia went to scratch Vino behind the ear, I reached for her elbow and started trying to lead her away.

"Hey!" the guy with the tooth grill said. "We were talking."

"Too bad," I said.

I dug my fingers into Sophia's upper arm and pulled her away from the guy.

"You can't do that, Sophia," I said, when we'd gone half a block. "The minute you open your mouth, people are going to think you're insane and they're going to take advantage of you."

"You told us to go turn tricks," Sophia said.

Two passersby heard Sophia and their heads swiveled in our direction.

I smiled at them.

"I was joking, Sophia. You were complaining about needing more weed. I can't afford to keep you three stoned for however long it is you plan to hang around. And, by the way, how long is that? Don't you have anywhere to go?"

"Go? Where the hell would we go? Back to the cemetery? We have no one. No friends. No relatives. No one. We've been dead for ninety years, remember?"

I sighed. "Right."

I'd barely closed the door to my apartment before Sophia kicked off the combat boots and started peeling off her clothing. Then, leaving the clothes in a pile by the front door, she tromped into the bathroom where I heard her start running a bath.

Annabelle and Birdie weren't feeling that ambitious. Both were lying on the sofa bed, looking piqued.

"Something is wrong with us," Annabelle said. Her eyes were puffy and her lips were cracked.

"Yes," I said. "You think you've been dead for ninety years."

"You don't believe us?" Birdie asked. "After all this?"

"After all what? It's not like you guys have walked through walls or started melting when sunlight hits your skin."

Annabelle seemed vexed. Birdie ignored me.

By ten a.m., their faces were the color of skim milk. They didn't have the strength to clamor, but were weakly begging for weed. I finally broke down and went around the corner to see Jeremy, my occasional supplier, the skate-punk kid who lives in a garage on Rope Alley.

"Whoa," he said, pushing his white-person dreadlocks out of his eyes. "You're really smoking it up, Zoey."

"I have houseguests."

"Oh yeah?" His eyes opened a little. "Female houseguests?"

"In a manner of speaking," I said. I was out the door with my new stash of weed before he had a chance to ask more.

I got the ladies good and stoned, and they did appear plumper and pinker after smoking. Then it was nearly noon and I had to go to one of my odd jobs, teaching yoga to developmentally disabled adults.

I changed into yoga pants and a tank top then washed my face and hands so I wouldn't reek of pot. I hadn't even smoked, but the zombies had exhaled all over me.

"You guys please stay inside the apartment and don't let anyone in. You can watch TV," I said, flicking on the television, which had initially scared the hell out of them, but now seemed to soothe them.

"Okay?" I glared at Annabelle.

She looked up at me, all dreamy and stoned. "Okay." she said in a faraway voice.

My dog was curled up next to Sophia, who was raptly staring at a talk show hosted by people wearing surgical scrubs.

The rec room where I teach the yoga class smelled like cabbage. Katie, a cheerful sixtyish woman, came bounding in.

"I brought you something!" she said brightly.

It was a dinosaur book. She had given me a dinosaur book the previous week too.

"Thank you, Katie."

Will, a tall man with a vacant stare, told me his back was hurting and he wanted me to arrange him into a restorative pose. I did.

The class went smoothly until one of the men peed his pants. I had to go find an aide who took him to get changed.

On the way home, I stopped at the coffee store, Swallow, and bought two pounds of coffee. That was another thing. The zombies liked their coffee.

As I let myself back into the apartment, I heard a male voice. My heart sank. Had Sophia gone out and found her friend with the tooth grill and brought him home?

The voices were coming from the kitchen. I walked in and nearly walked back out. What I was seeing was too fucking weird.

Doon, the neuroscientist acquaintance I'd e-mailed the previous night, was sitting across the kitchen table from Sophia, apparently drawing her blood. Doon, as far as I knew, lived in Pennsylvania and was not in possession of my street address.

"What are you doing here?" I asked.

"I came as soon as I got your e-mail," he said.

"Isn't that enough blood?" Sophia asked Doon.

I stared at the blood swirling around inside the syringe's cylinder. It was dark red, like any other blood.

"Almost," Doon said.

"What are you doing to Sophia?" I was feeling protective.

"Just drawing blood." Doon finally glanced up at me. "Hi, Zoey."

"Yeah. Hi," I said back.

Doon looked exactly as he had four years earlier when I'd helped look after his father: amiable, short brown hair, square jaw, deep-set black eyes, tidy clothing.

He started pumping the ladies for information. "What do you remember?" He was drooling in his eagerness to learn more about them.

Sophia was shaking her head, clearly not remembering anything, and Annabelle couldn't do much better, her earliest memory of her new life going back only as far as awakening inside her coffin as it was being split apart by the earth-moving machine.

"What are you going to test their blood for?" I asked.

"Anything that deviates from the norm," Doon said. "Ditto with their genetic material." He pointed at a kit containing giant Q-tips and glass slides.

I didn't like it. But the zombies were going along with it all. Presumably they were as eager as Doon to understand what they were.

It wasn't until he'd taken off, nearly two hours later, that I discovered Doon had given the ladies the creeps.

"The minute you left the room he asked questions that had

nothing to do with being dead," Birdie said. "Questions about life as a hooker. Dirty, nasty stuff."

Birdie was about as prudish as an undead hooker could be. Even one from 1924.

"Sorry," I said.

"Can we smoke now?" Sophia asked. "I don't feel well."

"Did you tell Doon that weed makes you feel better?"

"No," Birdie answered. "You said it's illegal."

"Right," I said.

I handed over my bag of weed.

My phone chirped early the next morning.

"Zoey," Doon said, "I'm assembling a team and we're coming up there. Your friends are most certainly over a hundred years old!"

"Really?" I mustered. I hadn't had coffee yet.

"*Really*. We will be up this afternoon. And we'll take over."

"Take over? *We?*"

"We're going to take your friends to the lab at Penn State."

"The lab? They're not rats, Doon. Not that rats should be in a lab either. But these are people. Or . . . something."

"We'll treat them respectfully and give them comfortable accommodations."

"What if they don't want to go?"

"What else are they going to do? Live on your couch forever?"

"I don't know, Doon, but I'm not sure they want to be experimented on."

"Zoey, this could be huge. If we can figure out what brought them back to life and what is sustaining their lives, well, imagine the implications!"

"Yeah, I guess."

"I'll see you later," Doon said, hanging up before I could protest.

I stared at my phone.

Alexander Vinokourov lifted his head, sniffed the air, then looked at me.

"They want to take them away," I said.

Vino blinked.

I tiptoed into the living room. They were still sleeping. I went into the kitchen, fed Vino, and put coffee on. Eventually, Birdie came into the kitchen and I offered her a few spoonfuls of Vino's meat.

She seemed surprised at my generosity.

"Why are you being nice to me?"

"What are you talking about? I'm always nice to you. I'm giving you shelter, food, clothes, and pot. What else do you want, a fucking kidney?"

"*Kidney?*" Birdie tilted her head.

Sophia and Annabelle made their way into the kitchen and started hovering. I waited till they'd gotten some coffee down then told them about Doon's plans for them.

"Pennsylvania?" Annabelle said, wrinkling her nose. "I was born there. I have no wish to return. Not even ninety-five years later."

"Does he think we're like Frankenstein or something? How horrible of him," Birdie said.

"Would we make money?" Sophia asked.

"It's possible."

"Would we go on TV?" Sophia pointed at the television set.

"Maybe," I shrugged.

"Really?" Sophia's eyes widened.

"Sophia, we do not wish to be put on display like zoo animals," Birdie said.

"We don't?" Sophia squinted.

"We don't," Annabelle said.

"Where can we go?" Birdie asked.

"Go?" I said.

"I don't want to be experimented on. If we stay here, they will come for us."

Birdie was right. But where could they go? They'd only been living in the twenty-first century for forty-eight hours. I couldn't very well send them to, say, Maine, or New Jersey, and expect them to blend in, never mind survive.

"What do you know about Wyoming?" I asked.

"Like your wallet?" Sophia pointed at my weed-stash wallet open on the coffee table.

"Like the state out west," I said.

"Cowboys?" Annabelle asked.

"Sort of," I said. "I think nowadays the cowboys drive pickup trucks and wear helmets. The West isn't that wild anymore, but nothing really is."

All three looked at me blankly.

"Well?" I said.

"What would we do when we got there? We have no money, no nothing," said Birdie.

"I'd get some odd jobs like I have here. And you would too."

They looked at one another. Then they looked at me again.

"Okay," Sophia shrugged. "I guess. But if it's horrible, then I want to go be a zoo animal and be on TV."

"How do we get there?" Annabelle asked, glancing all around, like maybe the twenty-first century had teleporting devices that she hadn't noticed yet.

"We'll drive," I said. "My car fits four. And a dog."

"When do we leave?" Annabelle asked.

"As soon as we pack up a few things," I said.

I had nothing I valued in the apartment. As for my jobs, the developmentally disabled adults wouldn't remember me for very long, and though I would miss seeing Henry, the big mastiff at the shelter, finally find a permanent home, it was about the only thing I'd regret.

What's more, I'd have company.

I'd always figured I'd eventually rescue more pit bulls or try living with a man for more than three weeks. Now, instead, I had zombies.

At least they had normal-sized heads.

Peter Cook

Bob Holman is a poet, professor, and proprietor of Bowery Poetry Club. His new book, his sixteenth (if you count CDs and videos, which he does), *Sing This One Back to Me*, is from Coffee House Press. His series on poetry and endangered languages, *On the Road*, is shown on LinkTV.org, and his new special, *Language Matters*, will premiere on PBS. He is also working on a multimedia performance called *The Trip*. Holman lives on the Bowery in New York City.

pasta mon
by bob holman

Pasta Mon cookin in a limousine
Windows rolled up—poem written in the steam
Poem starts to change—to a recipe?
I'm cookin up a story! You still hungry?

Deep in the blue sea deep in the memory
Connected, perfected—totally poetry
Yuppie got a puppy & the baby got a Pamper
Doin the 500 in a Winnebago camper

Why?
Why?
Why Pasta Mon cry?

Back in the history I shot the deputy
For not makin sauce sufficiently garlicky
Everyone entangled in a single ecstasy
A single strand of Pasta Mon's linguini

This is the wild life! Carbohydrates? Out of sight!
"Pasta Mon Fashions" give eyesight insight
See the world through spaghetti headlights
Ravioli figleaf? Pasta Paradise!

Why?
Why?
Fresh onions is why

So much pasta Mon cannot give it away
What's the matter with a platter of pasta pâté?
Keep the homefries burnin—a sorbet gourmet
You too can have your own authentic Pasta Mon beret

Pasta Mon starrin on his own tv show
Yesterday's menu's already obsolete-o
Today, I'll show you how to roll a pasta-filled burrito!
W/ no *habichuela* on the tuxedo

It might boil over—the pot is bubblin
It might boil over your mind that's troublin
It might boil over—dynamite!
Might boil away to nothin, spoil your appetite?

It happened to me while readin *Weekly Reader*
The future was comin—it would be beater
Beater. Deffer. Bigger forever.
Sun on the horizon—it was always risin

The Future is here—the Past is a goner
All stuffed in a pasta shell of once upon a
Time when the rhyme would be flora and fauna
A cheese syntheses: Utopian lasagna

A nickel for a can & a nickel for a bottle
A trickle-down sound from the nickel that bought you
America the Beautiful in quarantine
A cardboard mattress and a cardboard dream

Barbecue trash cans linin the Hudson
Dogs are howlin as you throw the spuds on
Pasta Mon's recipes gettin kinda smelly
Rat ratatouille & vermin vermicelli

It might boil over the pot is bubblin
It might boil over it's your mind that's troublin
It might boil over—dynamite!
Might boil away to nothin, spoil your appetite?

On the good ship *Pasta Mon*
Where the last macaroni is stuck to the pan
& the ship is sinkin
& the food is stinkin
& you just keep drinkin
O, oaweoh . . .

And remember!
"Bud" spelled backward,
. . . is "Dub"!

PART III
RECREATION & EDUCATION

Jesse Pesta

Cheryl Lu-Lien Tan is the New York–based author of *A Tiger in the Kitchen*. She was a staff writer at the *Wall Street Journal, InStyle,* and the *Baltimore Sun*; her work has also appeared in the *New York Times,* among other publications. The Singapore native has been an artist in residence at Yaddo and the Djerassi Resident Artists Program. She is working on her second book, a novel, and is the editor of *Singapore Noir,* a fiction anthology that Akashic Books will publish in 2014.

ganja ghosts
by cheryl lu-lien tan

The lousy bugger was taking so long to get ready that Jackson's balls really started to itch.

The tropical heat was so stifling, the scratchy polyester covering of the settee was so painfully glued to the bottom of his sweaty thighs, that Jackson wondered why he had bothered to come back to Singapore during the summer. He desperately wanted to scratch himself but he could hear Seng's mother shuffling about somewhere nearby. In the industrial-strength fluorescent light of Auntie's small living room, there was no hiding anything. After years of not seeing Seng or his mum—better to behave tonight.

"*Aiyoh,* my god . . ." Jackson mumbled, glancing at Richard, who was next to him on the sofa, tapping away on his phone, looking as fresh and talcum-powdered as he had an hour ago when they arrived at Seng's. Fucking irritating, Jackson thought. After just a few years away in the States, his body had forgotten how sweltering Singapore was when it wasn't monsoon season.

"Eh," Jackson said to Richard, who nodded, not taking his eyes off his phone, "what are we doing tonight?"

"Fucker," Richard responded, looking up and poking his third finger in Jackson's direction. "You don't remember, ah? Singapore, Wednesday night—nothing to do, *lah!*"

Seng's door opened suddenly, sending a blast of ice-cold air into the living room. *Bugger couldn't even share his bloody air-con,* Jackson thought. Seng, oblivious as usual, slowly made his way around the room, picking up his platinum TAG Heuer from the dining table and slipping it on his wrist, taking his keys off the hook next to the altar, then stopping to light a joss stick, bowing three times to his dad's grim face in a framed black-and-white photo before jabbing the incense in an ash-brimmed rice bowl.

"Eh—girls, stop complaining. Tonight is different, *lah,*" Seng said to his friends, tapping his hand on his chest pocket, stopping when his fingers found the shape of his lighter. "Ma," he shouted toward the kitchen as he reached into his back pocket for his Marlboro Menthol Lights, "we're making a move!" Sliding a cigarette between his lips so he could fire up the moment they left, he raised two fingers, gestured toward the narrow, chipped door, and started walking.

After all these years, the bugger still had the same *kwai lan* air he had even when he was fifteen. Whenever they walked into any room, whether it was a lecture hall or the front VIP section at Pump Room, Seng always swaggered ahead of the two of them, chest puffed out, chin slightly up, as he surveyed the place, watching people as they watched him, wondering who the fuck he was. Not that the three of them were a gang—but with Seng looking so *kwai lan,* Jackson was always on guard. If other guys thought they were some sort of gang or just trying to be fuckers, who knows where a staring contest could lead even in the most *stylo* of clubs.

"Richard, why must you be so negative?" Seng said, turning just slightly as he opened the door to make sure the other two were indeed scrambling off the settee. "Guys, tonight—don't worry. You just wait and see."

Jackson tried to keep up with Seng and Richard as they quickly shuffled down the three flights of stairs, puffing and flicking. Jackson had stopped trying to smoke in Chicago after a brief attempt, just to fit in with his colleagues at the insurance office. After some months of politely holding a cigarette and resisting the urge to gag while inhaling, he had decided to accept the fact that he was going to be the sad fuck left alone in the bar or at dinner whenever his colleagues went out to have a smoke. But Seng had given him such a look when he tried to explain that he didn't actually like smoking that Jackson just gave up and took one when Seng held out the box.

"Eh, seriously—where are we going?" Jackson asked again, wondering if he should have stayed home. His throat was starting to feel scratchy from the smoke and the heat. It was insane. Just because the three of them were best friends in secondary school didn't mean they still had anything in common. And Seng had always been crazy—god knows what he had in mind. Great—Jackson could feel himself sweating even more.

"Almost there, *lah,*" Seng said, breathing heavily as he darted between a few pillars and ducked into a narrow parking lot. "*Kau beh* so much!"

Jackson could start to hear the chipper hum of evening *kopitiam* chatter as they crossed the parking lot. Seng held his right palm out, asking them to wait outside the open-air shop when they arrived. Stamping out his cigarette with his shiny brown Prada sneakers, he smoothed back his gelled hair and sauntered into the heart of the coffee shop. How the guy managed to afford all this *atas* European-label crap on his shipping-company peon salary, Jackson had no idea. Even Richard had a much better job than Seng—some midlevel manager at Citibank or something—and he never wore any name-brand shit.

Jackson watched as Seng exchanged whispers, then a little cash and something else, with the *kopitiam* uncle. Uncle reached underneath his counter and pulled out six cans of Tiger beer and a few packets of chicken-flavored Twisties, putting them in a red plastic bag and handing that over. Seng shook the uncle's hand and slowly walked out. The whole exchange took less than two minutes. No one had even looked twice at them.

Seng was silent as he stepped outside, pausing briefly to light another cigarette before starting to move again, this time more quickly. Richard was quiet, texting as they walked, careful to keep his footsteps right behind Seng's. Jackson glanced around—the squat towers of cheap flats passed by slowly. There was a slender road before them, one of those old bus stops on the other side that looked like a faded, oversized orange mushroom, and next to that was a set of narrow stairs.

Ah, that's where Seng was going. The old place—a fortress of trees that was, at first, a good place to play hide-and-seek, and then later, a safe place to take girls in the early *pak tor* days. With all those trees around, who needs to spend fifty dollars at Hotel 88 for two hours of privacy? If the girls were enthusiastic enough in the park then, okay *lah*, worth it to spend the fifty at a hotel.

When Seng got to their old usual table, a chunky stone fixture with five short stools around it, he sat down, gesturing to Richard to open the beers, grunting loudly when the guy took a few seconds too long to set aside his phone. As Richard opened three cans, nudging one over to Seng and then Jackson, Seng yanked out a little plastic bag and a small flat pouch from his pocket.

"I make the first one, ah—but you better watch carefully." Seng pulled out a small piece of paper from the pouch, laid a few pinches of what looked like dried tea leaves on it, and started rolling. "This uncle here not going to roll all the ganja for you two lazy fuckers."

"Ganja?" Jackson said, almost shouting. "Are you crazy? We can get arrested, you know."

Richard jumped up, looking angry. "Oi—keep quiet! You want us to get caught, is it? You don't want to do, just fuck off, *lah!* Don't stay here and kill our mood." Seng just stared at Jackson, still holding the smoke in his hand. Richard sat back down, taking a long sip from his can.

It's not that Jackson had never done ganja—it happened once at a frat party at Loyola, on some drunken night when a cute girl had offered it to him and he felt he couldn't say no. He hadn't felt much of anything then, though—not from the pot or the girl. In the end he decided that, okay *lah,* at least he could say he'd tried pot once. Maybe better to just be a good citizen and call it a day. He never saw the girl again either.

"Fucker, how?" Seng said. "Want or don't want?"

The feeling was old and familiar to Jackson—trapped, mostly. A little exhilarated but trapped. Amazing how the years had passed, they were all thirty now, working men with real jobs, and Seng still managed to bugger him into all these things.

"Okay, okay," Jackson said. "But you start first."

Seng lit up the joint, took a deep puff, and inhaled, holding it in for a long moment as he passed the smoke to Richard, who did the same, then passed it over to Jackson. The joint felt warm between his fingers and he could smell its sickeningly sweet smoke. Jackson wasn't quite sure what to do.

"Oi," Seng said. "*Kani nah*—you not going to smoke then just pass it back, *lah,* okay? Don't waste."

Jackson put the joint between his lips and sucked deeply, holding his breath and trying hard not to cough. He passed the joint to Seng and the cycle started again. None of them said anything until the joint had made a few rounds, with Seng taking a last long puff before flinging it to the ground and grinding it out.

A cloud of deep, sweet air swaddled them now. Jackson was slowly exhaling, bit by small bit, trying to sense whether he felt any different. He heard a sharp squelch—Seng had opened a bag of Twisties and started loudly crunching away.

"Jackson, I tell you, ah, you been away so long, this country, ah—crazy already," Seng said. "You missed all these fucking stupid things! I tell you also, you won't believe."

"Eh, tell him about that guy!" Richard suddenly shouted, starting to laugh. "*Walau*—weird fucker, man!"

"So there's this guy, ah," Seng began, "apparently he can only *steam* about his wife when she's asleep. *Aiyoh*, so the fucker started drugging her at night, man—feed her sleeping pills all, so she's really still when he *pok* her! *Walau!*" He started laughing. "Like that, still okay. Weird—but okay. But then one night, the fucker wanted to really make sure she didn't wake up—their anniversary or some shit like that. So he tripled the dosage to make sure she really sleep deeply. But then, hello, the wife never woke up!"

Richard and Seng were laughing so hard neither could speak. Richard was doubled over, holding his stomach. Perhaps it was watching the two of them—or maybe the story? But Jackson heard himself starting to laugh too.

"I tell you," Seng said. "I told Richard, those people at wakes—better guard their coffins, man. Now that the guy's wife is dead and gone, he might start going to funerals to look for another dead girlfriend to *pok!*" Jackson was surprised to once again find himself whooping along with their laughter.

"Wait, wait—this one even more stupid, *lah*," Richard said. "Apparently, ah, there's this guy who got young, pretty mistress, *lah*. But then one day I think he want to break up with her or some shit. So apparently he met her by the side of some road to cut her off. *Wah*—the woman angry, man! She not only scratch his Mercedes and take off her high heel and bang it on the car and all. But then she started whacking him in the balls with her hands! Fucker just stood there with his head down, just accepting it!"

Richard had to stop for a moment until the mirth waned. "Wait—even worse. The whole thing—all caught on tape! Some guy passing by taped the whole thing on his iPhone then, *kani nah*, post on the Internet! *Wuahahahaha*—the rich fucker so embarrassed he can't even drive his ten-year-old son to school anymore, you know! The moment he show up, the parents, teachers, even his son's friends all laughing, *pointing pointing* at him for being such a no-balls fucker. This type of loser, better just do the world a favor and drown himself, *lah*."

Jackson had to wipe his eyes on his rolled-up sleeves. He hadn't laughed so much or for so long in many years. Could it be the ganja? Looking at Seng and Richard, clinking their beer cans now, he felt such love for them. How could he have wondered whether or not to come out with them? They would be brothers forever! He raised up his can and clinked it to theirs.

Seng started chuckling softly as he pulled out another piece of paper and began intently rolling. Richard opened a new packet of Twisties and passed it over to Jackson, who popped a few in his mouth and slowly chewed. He hadn't eaten Twisties in more than ten years—they were nowhere to be found in Chicago, for starters. But feeling the crunchy salty bits in his mouth and licking the yellow chicken-flavored dust off his fingers, he vowed to make sure he didn't go another ten years without eating Twisties.

"Guys," he said solemnly, "Twisties, I tell you, are really the best, man."

Seng looked at Richard, who looked back at him. Both of them directed a middle finger at Jackson and started giggling wildly again.

Jackson wondered if perhaps he'd had enough, but when Seng handed him the joint, he just took it and puffed. They grew silent, staring up at the glowing night sky and the skinny streetlamps nearby, sighing occasionally as they passed the joint around until it was dead.

In the sweet haze, Jackson felt himself getting carried along—chuckling at the rhythms of a life he had forgotten. He hadn't felt this free in ages—so open, so happy.

"This one—even more best," Richard said after a moment.

"Recently, ah, in Singapore, people all *kau beh* about this new homeless problem, *lah*. I guess, in recession, some people lost their homes or these foreign workers can't afford their cheap housing anymore, so they just sleep on those long stone benches at night. You look outside *kopitiams*, all also got one. So, government got no choice, *lah*—minister of home affairs make a speech, all, tell everyone don't worry, he has a plan. So, we all wondering, what is this plan? Put all these guys in a home? Or give them training, help them find jobs? Or what?

"Then one day," Seng continued, "Singaporeans woke up and went to their *kopitiams* for breakfast—and realized that, eh, very funny, but the benches all suddenly looked different. The government overnight had installed these metal arm dividers so now people cannot lie down! This is their brilliant plan, man—make the benches so uncomfortable that homeless people cannot sleep there anymore! Must find somewhere else to sleep. *Wah*, this one—really smart, man! In the government's eyes, problem solved."

This couldn't possibly be true! They had to be making it up. Jackson looked at Seng and Richard and just wanted to hug them. He couldn't ask for better friends. Why hadn't he moved back to Singapore? No one in Chicago made him feel as carefree and full as they did. He had never missed home before—after leaving for college in the States, his main mission had been to stay away from a world that had never quite made sense to him. He rarely thought about home, never felt guilty about not looking back.

"Eh, okay, one more," Seng said. "Then I take you to see something funny. Richard, tell him about the army guy—I need to take a piss."

As Seng wandered off toward some trees in the distance, Richard opened another three cans and passed one to Jackson. "Okay, there was this soldier, doing that compulsory military service shit, *lah*. Skinny guy, young kid. Apparently, one day on his way to reporting to duty, the guy was walking from his flat texting on his phone or some shit—and his scrawny maid is walking behind him, carrying his gigantic heavy army rucksack for him! The girl was so tiny that the rucksack was half her size and she was all bent over! Some other guy took a photo of this and posted it online—*wah,* crazy times, man! The photo went viral, everyone angry. The army had to launch investigation into who the no-balls soldier was, apologize all. Everyone laugh until crazy."

Unbelievable! Jackson was in hysterics now—he could hardly breathe. Seng, who had returned halfway through the story, was bent over and laughing too, even slapping Jackson on the back. Jackson didn't even care that the bugger had probably not wiped his hands.

Seng took his beer, downed the entire thing, crumpled the can in his fist, and said, "Come, we have to show you something." Richard and Jackson drained their beers as Seng rolled another joint, slipped it into his shirt pocket, then swept all remnants of their evening into the red plastic bag.

Seng didn't live far from Zouk, a nightclub that many teenagers and twenty-somethings packed on weekends when the three of them were kids. So when he started wending the familiar path that had taken them toward Zouk many a night after they'd spent a good hour at Seng's flat gelling up their hair and making sure their patterned silk shirts were untucked just so, Jackson knew where they were going.

"Eh, bugger, I'm not sure if I feel up for clubbing tonight," Jackson said.

"*Aiyoh*—just trust us, *lah,*" Richard said. His mood had shifted so much that he hadn't even pulled out his phone since they'd sat down. He and Seng were periodically erupting into giggles for absolutely no reason. "This one, you really must see."

When they got to the club, Seng walked to the front of the line packed with about fifty teens in miniskirts or drainpipe-tight jeans. He had a quick chat with the bouncer. When the man unhooked the velvet rope, Seng told the guys to follow him in, through a labyrinth of dark narrow hallways and up a flight of steps, toward a second-floor terrace overlooking the vast dance floor.

Leaning over the metal railing, the three of them mashed together, peeping down, just like they'd done in the past when they would play the which-girl-would-you-*pok*? game. (Only Seng had actually gotten lucky that way.)

"Look," Seng said, pointing toward the floor and the four raised cube podiums anchoring each corner of the large room, as the first beats of Belinda Carlisle's "Summer Rain" started up. The five hundred or so people packing the dance floor all started making the same hand gestures, entirely in unison—jazz hands fluttering downward for "rain," pointing toward their heads at the word "dream."

This might be what a North Korean military dance would look like, Jackson thought.

The precision dancing continued through "Square Rooms," and Bananarama's "Love in the First Degree," when, to their credit, the teens got slightly more emotive as they mimed the words, "*Guilty! Of Love in the first degree . . .*"

"Don't even try to actually dance to these songs," Seng said. "Those kids will push you off the fucking podium and spit on you for not knowing the right move." The three of them burst out laughing so hard they had to hold onto one another so they wouldn't fall onto the zombies below.

Seng pulled out a joint and lit it up. When Jackson looked worried, Seng pointed toward the crowd around them—everyone was smoking and ashing on the floor. "Smoking section," Seng mumbled, inhaling and then passing the joint to Jackson.

Soon they noticed a tall guy standing next to them. He had

nicely gelled hair and a small scar on his forehead. And he was staring at the joint that was now in Richard's hand.

"What you guys doing?" he said.

Richard ignored him, looking away.

"I not police, *lah*," the guy said, nodding toward Richard's hand. "Ganja, is it?"

Seng stared at him and the guy stared back calmly.

"Can I have a puff?"

Seng half shrugged and nodded, watching carefully as the guy took the joint from Richard's hand, put it to his lips, and sucked deeply. He had a quizzical expression on his face as he exhaled slowly. Then he took another puff.

"Oi! What you think you doing?" Richard shouted. "This one not cheap, you know!"

The guy ignored Richard, looking intently at the joint as he swirled the smoke in his mouth. Jackson could see Seng pushing up his shirtsleeves and standing up straighter.

Then, laughter. Not from Richard or Jackson and certainly not Seng. The wails of laughter were coming from the guy, who was actually stamping his feet.

"*Kani nah!* What the fuck is wrong with you?" Seng said, inching toward the guy.

"Me? What the fuck is wrong with *you*?" the guy countered. "This one not ganja, *lah*, you losers! This one just clove ciggies! What fucking idiots!" He threw the joint on the floor and walked off. Jackson could still hear the guy's laughter as he receded, even above the Rick Astley medley that had just started up.

Seng removed the pouch of leaves from his pocket and opened it, taking a few deep whiffs. He handed it to Richard, who spent a long minute smelling it.

Jackson suddenly felt tired. He turned around and leaned over the railing, peering out at the dance floor, at the army of robots, feet planted firmly, bodies unmoving as each of them made the same hand gesture to, "*Never. Gonna. Give. You. Up. Never. Gonna. Let. You. Down.*"

He couldn't remember what was funny about this. Or the army fucker who made his maid carry his rucksack. Or the government's solution to the homeless problem. Or the rich guy getting mocked by ten-year-olds over his mistress whacking his balls. Or the guy who killed his wife by fucking her in her sleep.

It was all just sad.

Beowulf Sheehan

Amanda Stern is the author of the novel *The Long Haul,* and the founder, curator, and host of the popular Happy Ending Music and Reading Series in New York City.

acting lessons
by amanda stern

The initial quantum fluctuation that burst forward to create this universe implanted particles programmed, in years nine to fourteen of a human girl's life, to flood the neural regions and saturate her suggestible self with one single, rabid desire: to become an actress. Why this specific link, no one knows, although recent scientific studies suggest a congruity: both teen girls and actresses embody a multiplicity of personalities, expressing each through overt behavior in narrow windows of time.

It was the first week of eighth grade and school was a cauldron of odors: fresh carpeting, new varnish, paint fumes, recently opened reams of three-hole-punch paper, just-sharpened pencils, wet presses of highlighter across textbook pages, ground meat and canned vegetables from the cafeteria, polyurethane coating the gymnasium floor, and the commingling, lingering off-gassing scent of back-to-school packaging. The notice board was wallpapered in greed, a pyrotechnic display of bubble-lettered pitches, business cards, and flyers, hatched by opportunistic adults eager to capitalize on private school kids, each blocking the other like tall kids in a class picture.

Assemblies were overbooked with presentations, a cattle call of adults trying to sell lessons that no one wanted. From Judo to gardening, our collective interest held steady at their resting rates, until the appearance of the young married couple straight from the pages of *Sweet Valley High*. Two tall tow-headed stalks synchronized down to their split ends, walked onto the school stage.

The angular pretty boy and his chisel-cheeked wife were the color palette of our dreams; the living, breathing incarnation of how we wished we looked, of the models we circled, tore from magazines, and brought to one hair salon after another, hoping each time, as we handed them the photos of Christie Brinkley and Carol Alt, that *their* salon would have the necessary supplies to cut off and bleach out our actual selves, providing us an opportunity which did not exist: to be replaced by preferred selves, now, specifically, the two expensive-looking fine-grain birch-totems on stage. Even their names sounded elite.

Ian and Caroline ran a theater company for teens; Caroline did most of the talking. She spoke fast and efficiently, like she'd not lost connection with her inner teen, but Ian was slower, he talked like he was inside a dream, and all the girls found him sexy. Three times a week the group met and wrote plays, performing them at the end of each semester. They were holding auditions and if we were interested, we should stay afterward and take a form. My friend and I exchanged knowing glances. We were going to audition for this theater company and we were going to get accepted because we were talented, damnit! Success was awaiting us; all we had to do was show up. Hell, I felt my future fame kicking from inside me like a drunken fetus. Had we known what "fee-based" meant, we would not have been so self-impressed.

My best friend Tea (as in Lipton, not Leoni) and I walked to the audition which was in a church basement on the Upper East Side, not far from our all-girls school. A curtain of teen stereotypes had staged themselves theatrically on the front steps. A cursory glance caught the stoner, the mean girl, the beauty, the gay boy, the fat kid, the metal head, the punk, the cut-up, the misfit, and the bored one. We knew these kids were the existing company, because they were intense; they smoked cigarettes with their souls. As we walked past them, Tea and I looked at each other; it wasn't tobacco they were smoking. It was obvious who was auditioning and who wasn't and Tea and I joined the other self-consciously asymmetrical faces, as we were assessed, surveyed, and scrutinized by the kids, willfully amnesic that they once were us—outsiders. No longer sandwiched between lady-suits and matching pearl sets, Ian and Caroline looked less different offstage. Embedded in their vow to serve as a platform for our fame was the promise that we'd become who they were—California and beachy-cool—but against the backdrop of the Lexington Avenue Christian Church, and Lexington Avenue itself, they didn't clash with the passersby rushing home to their classic six, in time to frisk their maids for stolen loot before day's end.

Caroline moved with the security of a rich girl; the swagger of knowing she could have what she wanted, and the entitled belief that she deserved it. Ian was the bad-boy pauper she spent her money trying to save. For a moment I was disappointed by what appeared to be a bait-and-switch, but that didn't last long. Ian reached out for the non-cigarette, and instead of stomping it out, he took a couple quick hits before handing it off to Caroline, who followed suit, returning it to the original kid. Tea and I had tried cigarettes, but never pot, and we were relieved that trying it now wasn't part of the audition.

We followed them inside to the atrium, where the regular company kids dropped to the floor in an automatic cross-legged circle we were urged to join. Tea and I shrugged. We'd never been to an audition before; we didn't know what to expect. Ian and Caroline removed their expensive jackets and joined the circle wanting to know all about us. Who *were* we? *Why* did we want to act? Had we had any prior experience? How was our home life? Did our parents treat us well? What were our struggles, our troubles, our demons? What pained us, and brought us shame? Trouble, they wanted us to understand, was the source of acting. Pain was the wellspring from which performance rose. The more we suffered, the better we'd be, and we were here to become the best, right? We *did* want to become actors . . . didn't we? The company kids stared at us and we nodded in the affirmative.

"So," Caroline said, "that's why you're here today. To tell us your story, to tell us who you are. Convince us, convince *me*, that you've got what it takes, that you deserve to be one of us."

Although I had an extended and confusing family—whose construct and evolution was so complicated I found myself relying on props and visual aids to make its form clear—I was not that bad off. I started out the youngest of three and when my father remarried and had children, I advanced to the middle of five, and when my mother remarried a man with three children, I was demoted to the youngest of six. Our lives were chaotic; my step-siblings had lost their mother and had moved downtown to live with us. They were angry, and often beat each other up, but without discipline there were no consequences, and without consequences the chaos escalated. It was easy to get lost.

I looked at Tea who, unlike me, was not frightened, but appalled, like someone who knew right from wrong. I scrambled for what I was going to say, while Tea looked at them like *they* were scrambled. The old kids went first, to show us the ropes.

"Hi, I'm Daniel, I go to Dwight, otherwise known as Dumb White Idiots Getting High Together, although they're not the ones I get high with," he said, tossing a laugh-and-glance to Ian, who either didn't see, or pretended not to. "Oh yeah, um . . . wait, what? Oh, right—my deal . . . My brother is gay and I wish he wasn't." A wash of realization spread across Daniel's face and he quickly looked over at a blond boy. "I didn't mean . . . Sorry, Jesse, you know what I mean, right?"

Jesse stared at his lap, and nodded yes.

"Anyway . . . I wish my brother wasn't gay because my parents take it out on me. And that sucks." Daniel turned to the squashed blonde sitting next to him and poked her. Out escaped a confused giggle.

"Oh! My turn!" She spoke in baby voice, and leaned her head onto Daniel's shoulder. "I'm Marcy. Daniel's my boyfriend so you bitches better stay away!" She laughed while glaring at the circle. "No, I'm kidding! *Of course* I'm kidding. Well, not about the fact that he's my boyfriend, he IS my boyfriend, but about staying away from him. No wait! I *do* want you to stay away from him . . . *Daniel!* Help me!" She blushed and shot an angry look at Daniel because he wasn't doing a thing to prevent Marcy from being herself. Caroline cut in.

"Morgan?"

"Hi. I'm Morgan." The boy was all monotone. "I used to live with my dad, but he killed himself so now I live with my mom, who's a drunk. Good times."

And on it went, and the nearer it drew to the new kids, the more horrified I became. Every confession offered up a perpetrator, the parent who wronged them, either physically or emotionally, but no one had anything wrong on the inside of them, like I did. And I never expected that one day I'd be forced to publicly expose my secret defects. That's precisely what made them secret—they were never to be revealed! Also, I wasn't entirely clear on what I had; no one was, which was precisely what made my issues so vexing. My first life memory is of the weird thing happening to me, and I knew, based on the mockery I received from my siblings and dad, and from the myriad doctors I visited, that it was not normal. I was born with a basketball net slung over my top ribs, and it was in there that the world dunked its balls of dread. When impending doom is your prominent emotion, there's no room to feel much else—for example, hope. My normal responses to normal things were abnormal. I reacted to temporary partings from my mother as though they were final. Every time I had to leave her for my father's house, or anywhere, I felt threatened with annihilation, an experience so fierce and real, it choked me, pricked me dizzy, conked my chest in, and made it hard to breathe. No matter how many times I left and returned, my body could not retain the part about returning. Each time was the first again, and several times a week I separated from my body, easily as an invertebrate from its shell, and slipped toward the ceiling, to watch, safe and distant as an omniscient narrator in a twentieth-century novel, my external self suffering the slow, sensational process of dying. It happened when I felt overwhelmed, when I was called on in class, when I had to take a test. When it happened in public, I had to control the internal hysteria, which meant I could not also engage in the world, and in those moments, depending on the circumstance, either I nodded my head, didn't speak, or left quickly. Sometimes I did all three. Fear and my reaction to fear created the reliable pattern that led my life and gave it shape, but no one beat me or locked me in closets, no one burned cigarette holes into my forearm or pushed me down uncarpeted stairs, and as the revelations rolled around the circle, I felt a twisted envy, awed by the traumas sustained by these kids, jealous that what Ian and Caroline wanted, these kids had to deliver.

When it got to Tea she rolled her eyes. She wasn't buying it. I didn't realize that not buying it was an option. She was cool and I was terrified. I had nothing to offer. As Tea started to speak, I felt myself grow dizzy, and begin to float away. My lungs were collapsing, deflating into flat shriveled tapeworms.

"Honestly, I feel sorry for all of you. Your lives totally suck. I'm not sure how this is supposed to make you a better actor. All it's doing is depressing me."

"You don't get it," Daniel said.

"Well, that's one thing we can agree on," she shot back, and turned to me with a big smile. "Your turn!"

My brain was all white noise and I felt caught in its fuzzy, thick middle. As they waited for me to speak, I heard a stomach grumble, a throat clear, legs reposition, a sniff, and its subsequent swallow. Their nervousness for me activated my concern for them, and in order to alleviate them of their discomfort, I had to say or do something, even if it wasn't what I meant to say or do. I felt my school uniform growing damp against my skin. When I shook my head *no,* I imagined myself in their eyes and decided never to return. I looked to the person next to me and said, "You go."

As the next person spoke, Ian stood, walked around the circle, and stopped at me. A moment later, I felt his hot breath on my neck.

"Hey, come with me a minute, okay?"

Another wave of heat and sweat careened through me as I stood, hoping my movements did not mirror the wild collapsing inside me. I followed Ian out of the room, on my two stale candy-stick legs, and into the main hall, prepared for the worst, knowing the impending humiliation would ruin my entire life, but not knowing exactly how. What he said to me, and how attentive he was, threw me so off-guard, swallowed me in such relief, that I didn't even bother to correct his incorrect assumptions. He thought I was hiding something, holding onto an enemy war code that he desperately wanted to break. He'd misconstrued my panicked *no* as a secret and I had a choice: maintain the mystery or come clean. While his misinterpretation of my withholding added validation to my concerns that I was always wrong and everyone else was always right, his intense focus triggered something bigger than my imminent fear. I got a hit of something I'd never tried and it swelled me with the best feeling I'd ever had. Unfiltered male attention; I wanted more. He put his hands on my shoulders and gave me a brief massage.

"You're tense," he said. "You need to loosen up."

When he finished, he slung his arm over my shoulder and headed us back to the atrium. "Maybe smoke a little weed. You've smoked weed before, right?"

"Of course," I said, all *duh* to override the truth.

And then he opened the atrium door and we walked back through it together.

Tea never returned, but I did. I liked acting, and I liked Ian, and while he had nothing to worry about, I wanted him to worry about me all the time. Each session started with the same group therapy, where I refused to speak, inciting more worry; except for his offers to find me weed, I was growing rather fond of his concern. After the late-afternoon teen confessional, the unoriginal, clichéd acting games and writing exercises, Ian and Caroline would take a cab to the village. Since I was the only kid member who lived downtown, they started offering me rides to their apartment on 12th Street and Sixth Avenue. I remember the very first cab ride because Ian said he was hungry for dessert. When Caroline asked what he wanted, he leered at her and said, "Boston cream pie."

She giggled and smacked him, and he winked at me, the forced conspirator, who was nearly certain, but not entirely positive, that she understood. They treated me as someone who already had life experience. On the other hand, they seemed eager to *be* my life experience. They never failed to remind me that I could call them at any time of day or night. If I needed them, if anything bad was happening to me, if I was in trouble, if my parents were hurting me, they were the people I should call. When weeks and months passed and I still hadn't called, their concern grew and their attention to me was amped so high, the other kids complained and I began feeling obligated to give them what they wanted. I was furious that my parents didn't pull out my hair or toss me from windows. How else would I be pushed to call on my volunteer saviors and have them rescue me like they wanted when no one was threatening me with harm?

A few months into the fall, Ian called me at home. He wanted to see how I was doing. I was doing fine. He detected an edge in my voice. No edge, I told him. I didn't have to pretend with him; I shouldn't feel the need to hide. Okay, I said, adding nothing. Whatever it is, I can handle it. Whatever is happening to you, I can help you. I've been there before. What do you mean? I asked. My parents, they hurt me too. What do you mean? I asked. I mean, you're not alone, runt, he said. (I was hurt by the term "runt" but tried not to spiral into an unhinged insecurity by reminding myself of Wilbur, the lovable pig in *Charlotte's Web*—also a runt!) I know your pain. I see what's happening to you. You do? I asked. I do, he said. I wanted him to tell me what he saw, because I needed material in order to have something to tell him. His calls became frequent and so did his questions. He even started coming over. Whenever I mentioned a guy, he'd ask me if I'd slept with him.

"Howard Jones?" I'd asked, incredulous. "I wish."

No matter how many times I responded no, I hadn't slept with him or him or him, or anyone for that matter, he continued to ask me. I either did not get it, or didn't want to get it. A journal entry from that time validates both assumptions:

> *Ian came over yesterday. He's so weird. He's always asking if I've had sex with this person, this person, etc. I just wanna scream in his ear, Ian, you fuck—I'm a VIRGIN! That would shut him up for about five minutes.*

Ian wanted something from me I could not name and I wanted something from him that I could: a father. That's all I wanted. I had always been drawn to older men. Since I was mini, I'd tried co-opting every grown man I came into contact with: our poor carpenter, a random babysitter, a few camp counselors, and, most recently, the acting teacher. In turn, the attention they paid me was driven by their needs, which were in opposition to mine, but that never prevented me from slipping under the open wing of a spare man. It took only a few months before I was rolled up in Ian's.

I didn't know what he wanted from me, but I liked that he wanted anything at all, and people pleaser that I am, I was determined to give it to him, which meant becoming the person he assumed I was. Were I to fail, hit a false note, reveal myself as anything other than the dark, intense, fucked-up girl he was coaxing out of me, then I'd be the wrong type of girl for him and he wouldn't want a thing from me at all. While I did have dark and intense feelings and struggled with real emotional issues, including an unfeminine reserve of anger, Ian was tugging at a part of me that already existed, but probably never would have developed had I not met him. And in his presence, I played the part of the brooding female James Dean, saying all the troubled things I knew he wanted me to say, as a dizzy-hot spray swept over every lie I told. I was in over my head and I did not know how to extract myself. I had no self yet, I was too young, so while I knew I wasn't being me, I didn't know how the person who *was* me acted. I simply knew she wasn't this way. But I could not release Ian into the world so that he could find another fourteen-year-old girl to dote on. I did not want his focus on me to disappear, and I knew it would if I disappointed him by not being the fucked-up mess he desperately wanted to save. And that is when my lessons in acting truly began.

The truth is, I *was* fucked up. Genuinely and authentically troubled, but had I been given a bit more time to articulate the mess inside, I'm fairly certain I would have expressed it differently.

Without having someone for whom I was curating my inner

life, I feel I would have found a more positive and productive way of expressing myself. My parents didn't abuse me and yet I felt abused. I wasn't adopted and yet I felt adopted. I knew I existed and yet I didn't feel seen, and now someone not only *saw* me, but wanted to be my hero, and I had *always* wanted a hero. I had longed for such a thing my entire life and here he was, a handsome man nearing thirty waiting for someone like me to save.

One night after class, Caroline and Ian invited me upstairs to their apartment. It smelled like Irish Spring and toast. They offered me a soda, told me to relax on the couch, and then Ian pulled out a bag of pot and looked at me.

"I told you I'd come through for you," he said, handing it to Caroline, who began to roll a joint. I panicked, looked at the clock, and pretended I had to get home.

"Like anyone will even notice you're not home," Ian said.

Right. Right. That. I had forgotten that my home life was one of utter neglect. That I could be gone for days and no one would notice. I had not kept track of every lie, of the labored-over poems and fake diary entries I left in places he could conveniently find. I had designed an entire mise-en-scène that wasn't physically true in any apparent way. I had covered the gaping hole of truth with falsehoods and now I was falling through one.

I was trapped. Caroline lit the joint, and when she was done, passed it to Ian, and after he was done, he handed it to me. I took the joint and the requisite drag, but coughed hard on the exhale sending ripples of laughter through them, which sent a fire of fear up my entire being. Had I fucked it all up? I handed it back to Caroline and then motioned to the clock and the door again.

"Oh, please, you can smoke a little more," Ian said, handing the joint back to me. I had no choice; I had to smoke more pot. After another hit, a sweat-inducing nausea began to rise, alerting me that something ominous was about to happen. Then I felt it, a tickle in my throat, which I tonsiled back, trying hard to trap it, but it couldn't be squelched. Nothing was more embarrassing than allowing my actual truth to escape in front of these people. A cough, or god forbid a sneeze, anything suggesting bodily susceptibility, had to be blocked at the pass. Perhaps because I was playing a part and concealing my human self, I began to feel not human, as though I was as biologically different from my body as my persona was to my reality. I had such control over my performance, my nuanced expressions, and body language that a natural function, such as a cough, threatened to topple the entire empire. The only way to get beyond the moment was to move past the cough, and the only way to move past the cough was to cough, which I did, seemingly without end.

My hope was that the cough would scratch the tickle and send it away, but it did no such thing. If anything it seemed to thicken it, morph the tickle into an object, something lodged, like a bone or a seed had wedged itself into one of my tonsils. This something was not sliding down, would not pass, and through the coughing, my fear escalated that I was going to vomit, choke on my vomit, and die. The last thing I wanted to do was die in front of the two people I was trying to impress. Was I allergic to pot? Had smoking brought this on? Was coughing like this a secret symptom of someone who had never smoked pot before? Were they on to me now because I was unwittingly giving away my secret? I could not stop coughing. I was dying. I was doing the most embarrassing thing a human could do. Dying was a secret you tried to keep. At fourteen you don't know enough about life to understand that dying is as ugly as living. I had presented myself to them as invincible and if I actually died now, they'd know that I'd been lying. I didn't want to disappoint them, even after I was dead!

Caroline handed me a glass of water, which did not help and I knew I had to leave, to get out before the unseemly and weak process of dying began and I lost control over my bodily functions and vomited, peed, and diarrheaed right there on their freshly waxed and polished hardwood floors.

I felt the familiar loop begin: sweaty palms, tightening chest, the dizzy beginning of floating away. I had to get out of there and I managed to look at my watch and make an excuse I can't remember, forcing myself away and out. On the street I could breathe a bit better, but a block or so later I was swept up again and there I went, into the city trash, head over pissed-on piles of paper and Styrofoam cups, throwing up my entire day. When I was finished, I turned and looked up to their building, worried I'd catch them watching me from behind their ninth-floor window, but they were not. I worried that they'd pass this garbage can and know that this was MY vomit. I walked home, but knew I was really stoned when the blocks became less and less familiar and I worried that I'd entered a part of the world that did not exist, that existed when you took the only wrong turn no one had yet taken, but of course I had taken it because that's just the kind of luck I had. When it finally occurred to me to look at a street sign, I realized I'd been going the wrong way. I couldn't manage to get anything right, not walking home stoned, not getting stoned.

I threw up several more times on my way home, and when I got there, I spun in bed until the morning, where I woke up into a hot cloud of shame. I was determined to change, to become a person who smoked pot easily, without coughing or throwing up, or fearing they were dying. I just had to practice, was all. I had to practice out of Ian's range; I had to do what I'd said I'd already done, which was smoke a lot of pot. I had to make good on my lie by wrangling my present to double as my past, until I was such a seasoned pot smoker that my claim would become retroactively true. In order for a lie to become the truth, you must make it your priority. The time you have between lying and getting caught is limited and if you don't take control of the situation, locking in a masterful timetable, you're screwed.

Daniel smoked pot. I could practice with him, without letting on that our smoke-outs were technically dress rehearsals.

Turns out, he was totally game. When he came downtown with the practice pot, I felt confident in my ability to overcome my first-time reaction. I studied him as he rolled the joint, determined to master that next. He lit up, took a deep drag, and handed it off to me, before lying down to stare up at the sky. We passed it back and forth until a creeping horror began to rapidly spread inside me. It was happening again; this time was worse. I was being squeezed from the outside by the atmosphere and couldn't breathe no matter where I stood, and that's when I realized that *this* was true dying, which is why I became suddenly religious and excused myself for the bathroom where I went to vomit and pray. I did not like smoking pot. It made me die. It was actually killing me at that very moment. How was I going to fake this? Actors relied on fake props all the time, but for the life of me, I couldn't figure out how I was going to finesse a false inhale.

I lived in fear of going back to Ian and Caroline's place, but I could only stay away for so long without having to provide some sort of believable excuse. I came up with one-liners for when he pulled out a bag of weed. None had traction. I couldn't "already be high" when we'd been together all afternoon. I couldn't be "trying to quit," because no normal teenager in the prime of her pot-smoking years makes a measured decision to scale back her drug use.

When I did return to their apartment it was for a party. I assumed all the kids would be there, but Daniel and I were the only ones. I was overwhelmed by all the "adults" but Daniel was used to them, he even knew their names, and he knew what Ian wanted when he asked to "borrow" him. When they returned, Ian "borrowed" me. He brought me down the hall to the bathroom.

"You've done coke before, right?"

I quickly rewound the tape of all the lies I'd told him but was unable to recall all the drugs I'd lied about doing.

"Yeah, obviously," I said.

He smiled, took my hand, and slipped something into it. "Have fun."

In the bathroom, I looked at the object and while I knew it was a vial (I recognized it from the street), I had no idea what I was supposed to do with it. How much coke was normal for a person to do? I opened the vial, shook a little out, turned on the faucet, and rinsed it down the drain. To be safe, I emptied a little more and when I cleared the sink basin of the granulated remnants I returned to Ian and Daniel and handed it back. Ian investigated.

"Wow. You're a fiend," he said. "Nicely done."

"Thanks," I told him, accepting a beer.

The next time I went over to their apartment, it was with Ian alone, who had a "surprise" for me. I was afraid. But each time I stepped into the persona side of myself, the more in control I felt, as though the strange things happening inside were happening to her and not to me. The more time I spent playing this dark part of myself, the farther down I pressed the real me. Truth is, I much preferred this other me, the tough-girl, punk, no-bullshit, nothing-can-hurt-me, my-family-is-more-fucked-up-than-your-family attitude, than I did the scared girl who was, well, frankly, a baby.

Ian, it turns out, was impressed with my aptitude for doing coke, and as luck would have it, the baggie he held up didn't contain pot, it contained powder. He wanted to do two things with me, he said—get me into a bathing suit and "do blow," something I'd done a million times, of course, as evidenced by last week's party. There was no getting out of this. I had to do it. I watched everything he did. The way he chopped that little block of hardened powder into loose mounds, and separated them into military lines. He had a straw he'd cut and he put it under his nose and over the coke and vacuumed away the troops. My turn.

Coke, it turned out, was just my speed (sorry). It knew me better than I knew myself. It made me more hyper, more vigilant, more masterfully in control of my body and self. There was no impending death, no fear, no conviction of my weakness and failings. In fact, I was invincible. Even my lies felt true. I never smoked pot with Ian again. He'd given me an out, and the out was coke. Every time he rolled a joint, or held up a bag of pot, I'd say, "Kid's stuff."

And so, with Caroline's money, Ian funded our seemingly endless supply of cocaine. He'd pick me up from school, drive me to Caroline's country house without her knowing, make me prance around in a bathing suit, attempt to talk me through giving blowjobs and handjobs, and began telling me how psyched he was for me to turn eighteen.

"Why?" I asked him.

"Because then I'll be legal to fuck you."

I was flattered he thought we'd still be friends in four years, but I was also terrified. I was more afraid of sex than I was of death. What was I going to do in four years? How was I possibly going to get out of that? Short of cutting him off forever, I hoped four years was long enough to strategize a master plan.

We spent the next four years inseparable, and the catalog of unacceptable behavior started to feel acceptable, but the closer I got to eighteen, and the more he reminded me about what was going to happen when I got there, the more panicked I grew. The day I graduated from high school, I stopped going to the acting school, and I stopped returning his phone calls. I never spoke to him again. He's tried contacting me twice. The last time was a few months ago, through my website. Here is the letter he sent me:

From: IAN
Subject: Hello Old Friend

Hello Amanda, Wow What a trip to see how great your career is going. how are you? Just thought It's been a long time since I saw you last, a lifetime really. Just wanted to say Hi and maybe we can catch up on life.

I'm very proud and quite impressed with your accomplishments. I hope to hear from you soon.

p.s. Don't freak out about this. Always your friend, Ian

One last thing. After a treacherous few months when I was twenty-seven, I was finally diagnosed. Turns out things did happen to me that didn't usually happen to others. I had panic disorder and there were drugs, that were not cocaine, to treat it. While I seldom have panic attacks anymore, I still feel a tugging anxiety at the sight of preteen girls and the men who pay attention to them. It's only now, when I look at those full, baby-fat faces that I have perspective and can see with objectivity how morally despicable Ian was to prey on me. I feel sad for Caroline and I even feel sad for Ian, but I feel sadder still for their baby girl, born fourteen years ago, and the age now that I was when I met him.

Jan Folsom

Jan Heller Levi is the author of *Once I Gazed at You in Wonder,* which won the Walt Whitman Award of the Academy of American Poets. "Eve Speaks," included in her second collection, *Skyspeak,* won the *Writer Magazine*/Emily Dickinson Award of the Poetry Society of America. Her next book, *Orphan,* will be published in 2014 by Alice James Books. Levi is also the editor of *A Muriel Rukeyser Reader;* served as consulting editor for the new edition of Rukeyser's *Collected Poems,* and is currently working on a biography of Rukeyser. With Sara Miles, she coedited *Directed by Desire: The Collected Poems of June Jordan.*

ethics class, 1971
by jan heller levi

Don't be frightened, Mr. Bliss said, we've got
to talk about these things. You can be honest—

how many of you have experimented
with drugs? Mr. Bliss was cool. So, okay,

about half of us, shifting in our seats, sneaking
looks at one another, slowly raised our hands.

An hour's discussion ensued about pros and cons,
and sure, the moral issue. Yes, it's true, Mr. Bliss

agreed, Thoreau said you *should* break a law
you don't believe in, but didn't he also say the body

is a temple, that the gift nature gives us is
to be shown matter, to come in contact

with rocks, trees, wind on our cheeks!
the *solid* earth! the *actual* world! There were

half-decent questions asked, and answers
none of us took too seriously. And when the hand-raisers

got home that afternoon, we'd each been nailed
by a phone call from school. It wasn't so bad

for me, my parents already knew I was rotten.
But Jamie got the shit beaten out of her,

Stan's parents shipped him off to military school.
Wesley gave up pot for drinking; in April he drove

himself into a tree. Through the rest of the year,
Mr. Bliss continued to pose interesting questions—

If a baby and a ninety-year-old both fell off a ship and you
could only save one, which would it be? Your mother's

sick, you have no money for her medicine,
Would it be wrong to break into the pharmacy

and "borrow" it? What about risking
the life of one to save the lives of many?

For our final—stoned on some primo hash,
I wrote a B- essay on honesty.

Rachel DeSario

Josh Gilbert is a documentary filmmaker and writer. He currently resides in New York City with his girlfriend and their son Henry.

the devil smokes ganja
by josh gilbert

It was in the mid-1990s when the famous Godfrey Jackson walked into my office wearing his vintage dreads and Birkenstocks and asked me if I could help his daughter Gladys land a job in the film industry. It wasn't as if Jackson didn't have the connections necessary to help her find a job—he surely did—but he didn't want to call in a favor and risk rejection based on some old industry beef or an unpredictable blindside. As Jackson spoke, he slouched down into his chair across the desk from me, and being the ever-sycophantic aspiring junior executive that I was, I eased into a slouch to mirror his and begged him to please continue.

He told me Gladys had just returned to the US from Russia where she'd been studying existential Russian poetry at the University of Kiev and was lost back in Los Angeles and always had been. Being the daughter of a celebrity was never easy, and Gladys had turned her Freudian angst into sexual promiscuity, while her brother Munsey had developed a nasty mean streak and an unruly belligerence.

I was relatively new to the business at the time, a recent film school graduate, driving around town in an old wreck of a BMW with no money to fix it—your typical big-hat-no-cattle film industry hack with a total of three midlevel connections that I milked for everything they were worth. With a cocky reassuring nod, I told Jackson I'd see what I could do.

"Thanks, mon," Jackson said, "I'll have Gladys give you

a call." He ambled out of my office, leaving me slouched in my chair, wheels churning about how to find the girl a job.

Jackson had been directing, starring in, and producing a self-financed film that our production company was line-producing called *You Best Shut Up!* about an unemployed bicycle mechanic with the IQ of a cabbage, who rides off on a journey in search of Life's Greater Meaning. Like most of Pepperpot and Jackson's comedies from back in the day, the flimsy story line did little more than serve as an excuse for audiences to laugh at the mishaps of a pot-addled idiot while smoking themselves into oblivion.

I'd been a huge fan of Pepperpot and Jackson comedies since I was a kid and was starstruck from the moment Jackson had walked into my office. Now, don't get me wrong, I'm no celebrity ass-kisser. Far from it. I grew up in one of LA's storied canyon communities, lousy with big-name entertainment industry icons, all milling about at the local food mart. But Pepperpot and Jackson had that seminal impact on me as a kid that wields the ultimate influence on any fan—a history of preadolescent enthusiasm bordering on obsession. And while Jackson's fortunes were way down at this point in his career, during their heyday, the comedy team had amassed a monumental following of ticket-buying enthusiasts and potheads.

Several days later, Jackson's daughter Gladys called me, and for the next few weeks we wound up spending many late nights together, sometimes wearing clothes but mostly naked, with me giving her pointers on script analysis, and after several Bacchanalian all-nighters, I became unequivocally convinced she had what it took to truly succeed in Hollywood, and with a concerted effort and a little luck I managed to land her a job interview with Cecil B. Glazer's production company. It was a relatively easy thing to do because Gladys was bright, beautiful, and sexually uninhibited, and Cecil was the cad son of a billionaire with a weakness for nymphomaniacs. When Gladys got the job, Godfrey Jackson was thrilled.

It was at this time that Jackson was becoming totally obsessed with catching up to his former partner and arch nemesis, Aaron Pepperpot, who had leveraged his post–Pepperpot and Jackson comedy career into a solo one by starring in a series of hit films and prime-time television shows. As Pepperpot's stock rose and Jackson's fell, people in the industry openly opined to Jackson's face that Pepperpot had always been "the funny one."

When my company organized a screening of Jackson's *You Best Shut Up!* at a prestigious theater on Hollywood's Walk of Fame, the venue was filled with studio heavies, a smattering of B-list celebrities, and his former sidekick Pepperpot, who had played a bit part in the movie as a professional courtesy to Jackson. Jackson had made a lot of people a lot of money over the course of his career and even though the chances were slim he'd do the same thing on his own, this savvy crowd knew the possibility existed, however remote, that he could be the next big Hollywood rebound story.

But not this time. Each bad joke on screen elicited a groan from the audience, soon followed by the disruptive rustling of people heading toward the exits. As the theater emptied out, it became painfully obvious that redemption had once again eluded Godfrey Jackson. When the curtain closed and the lights came up, Pepperpot gave Jackson a condescending pat on the back, said, "That's show biz!" and walked out of the theater with a look on his face that could only be described as schadenfreude.

Several months later, with the corpse of *You Best Shut Up!* still warm, Jackson was back in my office once again, this time proposing that we cowrite his next screenplay. His wife Leona, who called all the financial shots in the family, agreed to pay me a small per diem, which would be deducted off the top of the sale price when the script sold. And it would sell. Jackson was certain.

At the time, I was on a corporate career path, and not enthusiastic about the prospect of living an untethered existence, sipping lattes at the local coffee shop, cooking up the next shortcut to greatness; Jackson was offering me a life of creative self-direction. This wasn't a devil-may-care date with destiny. This was *a calculated risk* and I actually believed in Godfrey Jackson's talent and ability, that he could tap into a gigantic audience with the right creative content. And that's where I came in.

Even though it had been years since any of Jackson's solo efforts had shown a profit, he was still convinced a studio would give him twenty million dollars to make *our* movie, as long as it was mainstream enough to capture the hearts and minds of the next generation of twelve-to-eighteen-year-olds. And so, with this core demographic as our Holy Grail we developed an outline for a comedic screenplay about a black guy named Delray Johnson—a character we specifically wrote for Eddie Murphy—a crass, street-smart con man who is mistaken for Asian when he smokes pot and gets tangled up with a bunch of weed smugglers from Hong Kong. Antics ensue.

Initially, I found the entire premise offensive and racist, but Jackson said my "politically correct" resistance was proof positive that I was a closet racist, because any comedian with an ounce of credibility knows that racism is a *reality on the street* and that comedy isn't funny unless it's real.

We called the screenplay *Hong Kong Bong Song.*

I was totally committed to writing a saleable screenplay, putting the legendary Godfrey Jackson back on the map, and getting on the map with him. He may have been a block of ice in Hollywood, but to me he was still the coolest guy who'd ever lived and I couldn't get enough of his Horatio Alger rags-to-riches stories. He told me all about his early days growing up dirt poor in the mixed-race, working-class Pittsburgh suburb of Homestead, raised by a heroin-addicted hooker grandmother who rode with a biker gang and was famous around town for giving the best toothless BJs in the history of whoring. Jackson also gave me endless dish about Pepperpot, the son and grandson of executioners at a state penitentiary in Georgia—not your typical Pepperpot and Jackson audience members. And that "Pepperpot" had grown up as "Aaron Buckley Montgomery" in a middle-class suburb and had never even seen marijuana, let alone smoked it, before meeting Jackson, the true root-ball of their successful nine-year pot-fueled run.

Yet no one in the Hollywood mainstream really gave a shit about truth or authenticity. To the industry, where perception is everything, Pepperpot was the winner and Jackson was the loser, one notch above your average one-hit wonder.

The more time I spent with Jackson, the more I realized how lost and hopeless he was, and I began to focus all of my creative energies and professional ambitions on propping him up and convincing him he had the goods to make his way back onto the big-dog grid. Pepperpot and Jackson movies and records had made their distributors boatloads of money. With the right property, I was certain these same shark operators would welcome Jackson back into the tent with open arms. As for his low-trading stock as a comedic actor, there was no denying his legendary history as a performer. The same thing had happened to Frank Sinatra, had it not, and Elvis? Former megastars who had crashed and burned and were all but forgotten before rising out of the ashes and achieving new heights. No question, Jackson was just one project away from celebrity redemption!

After several weeks of slogging our way through the first draft of our screenplay, Jackson noticed I didn't seem the least bit interested in smoking pot—and the thing people talked about when they met Godfrey Jackson was pot. They'd launch into their "unique" stories about how the first time they ever smoked marijuana was listening to *How High Are Ya??* or watching *Big Beef*

Bong-O in their big brother's bedroom. To fans, Godfrey Jackson was the human embodiment of pot.

This added to my appreciation of his underdog comedic legacy; but in truth, pot didn't interest me. I was too "uptight," he said, and frankly, I was getting on his nerves with all of my talk about Sid Field and Aristotle.

I'd smoked pot a couple of times in college, though it wasn't something I ever really thought about. But when Jackson decided I needed to get high to free up creatively and invited me to join him in a toke, I consented.

Jackson took a small stash box out of his cabinet, plucked out a choice bud, and packed it into the glass bowl of his bong. It was dark, almost black ganja, which I later learned was the legendary "Lamb's Bread" from Jamaica—the all-natural gold standard of the outdoor, pre-Kush, genetically enhanced, hydroponically produced seed varietals.

Jackson smiled impishly at me as he lit the bowl and took an epic hit, keeping the smoke in his lungs with several short sucks of air for what seemed an eternity. Just when I thought he couldn't possibly hold the smoke any longer, he sucked it back down into his lungs again and held in a cough with a grunting, sipping sound, waited for several seconds, and then finally blew the smoke out, nodding sagely my way, eyebrows raised. Then he handed me the bong. I held it apprehensively and watched the glowing red bowl of burning black bud from across the upper lip of the water pipe, and with Jackson watching, I slowly inserted my face into the bong hole, lips first, hit the Bic for good measure, waved it lightly across the already burning bud embers, and sucked in an enormous, seemingly endless quantity of gray THC-laden fumes. Then, following Jackson's lead, I held it in my lungs for as long as I could, which in my case was about two seconds, tried to suck it back down again but couldn't handle the pressure in my lungs, and coughed spasmodically, sending a prodigious plume of smoke into the room. I gasped for several seconds and then coughed and coughed and coughed before finally regaining my composure and realizing, almost instantly, that I was *extremely* high.

Jackson smiled knowingly as he shelved the bong, and without a moment's hesitation began to riff mad comedy off the cuff with giddy, inebriated abandon as I typed away. As usual, I had no idea what he was talking about, but whereas before I might have resisted his humorous impulses as tedious or unfunny or just downright lame, now his goofy humor sounded like the funniest shit I'd ever heard in my life! I laughed and laughed as his hairy face lit up and he said, "We're going to hit the jackpot with this one, mon!"

When I went home that night I was still high. The next morning, as I spent an hour spreading peanut butter on a piece of toast, I realized I was *still* high. I know it sounds implausible, but I was high for an entire week. I went to sleep high. I woke up high. Each day I drove from my little house in Venice, California, up along Pacific Street and down California Street, onto the Pacific Coast Highway and up the winding coastline to Topanga Canyon, then up the mountain pass to Jackson's house, nestled behind a gigantic grove of big bamboo, all the while high as a goose.

Meantime, Jackson was right. For the final stretch of our writing effort, the pot loosened me up. It probably didn't make the script any better but it certainly made me think it was funnier, and soon we had finished *Hong Kong Bong Song.*

We were both confident the script had turned out well, so we organized a reading with ten of our friends, mostly mine, put joints around the room next to a plate of pot brownies, and laughed our asses off from fade-in to fade-out. After securing the rabid enthusiasm of our core demographic—the incredibly high—we went to market with a pot comedy disguised as a mainstream comedy.

Jackson called some of the most powerful decision-making executives across the painted hills of Hollywood and gave them "the opportunity" to read our script, but after several weeks of deafening silence it became clear that no one was going to give us twenty million dollars to make it. In fact, no one showed even the slightest interest in optioning the script, which *is* pretty funny (and still available). But the experience solidified our friendship—and I developed a lifelong affinity for good bud.

Years later I was living in New York City, where I'd moved to become a "serious writer," which is to say a seriously unemployed writer. It was a year after 9/11 and the world as we Americans knew it had changed forever. The Patriot Act had just passed through Congress and was signed into law by the Bush administration; the terrorist threat facing the nation was quantified daily by degrees of color on charts and graphs; neighbors who you'd never met suddenly wanted a peek up your ass crack to see if you were packing a dirty bomb. New York City's social anonymity suddenly became a thing of the past, with the harsh light of fear-driven paranoia casting ugly shadows in every direction.

It was against this backdrop that I sat down one morning to enjoy my daily ritual of black coffee, a toasted bialy, and the *New York Times,* when I noticed an article above the fold on the front page announcing the arrest and deportation of Godfrey Jackson. The story reported that Jackson had been apprehended in his Topanga Canyon home by federal agents and immediately deported to the storied detention camp in Guantánamo Bay, Cuba, for being a "Drug War terrorist," an "enemy combatant," and for being, most critically, an "illegal alien" (which qualified him for his stint in Guantánamo).

The newspaper story gave the details of the government's preposterous assault, which featured several hundred armed agents descending on Jackson's hillside Topanga mansion wielding assault rifles, billy clubs, and stun guns. Apparently, when Jackson confronted the commandos, demanding to know the charges, they zapped him in the groin with a stun gun, threw him twitching into a large burlap sack, and flew him straight to Guantánamo.

The federal agents informed his flustered wife Leona and their belligerent son Munsey that Godfrey Jackson had spent his life promoting the use of marijuana and by doing so had been identified by the office of the attorney general as an "illegal terrorist alien"—and because he was not a citizen of the United States he would be held in a steel mesh cage, exposed to the elements for "as long as it takes," and all the while surrounded by "towel heads" with an affinity for "back-door action."

Sending Jackson to Guantánamo for being an illegal alien was an outlandish act, perpetrated by a too-big-for-her-boots US attorney who, like most US attorneys in the history of US judicial overkill, was solely intent on making a name for herself, in this case during the nation's heightened War on Terror, by getting Jackson to do a "perp walk."

There was just one catch in the brilliant US attorney's otherwise flawless prosecution: Jackson was *not* an illegal alien. He was born in Homestead, Pennsylvania, in the Jewish suburb of Squirrel Hill; he was a US citizen, and could prove it. His grandmother and parental guardian may have been a scandalous, toothless hooker, but she was also born in Pittsburgh and she had the paperwork to prove it.

Initially, these facts didn't make a difference to the US attorney, who had pursued Jackson's prosecution with a relentless, feverish intensity for the better part of two years, spending a whopping $136 million of government funds in the process. She and her team had acted "well within the law," she announced during her makeshift press conference in the Guantánamo Bay rec room to a smattering of press corps. Besides, the government's action was by its very nature de facto "extrajudicial," ergo she could do whatever she damn well pleased and if anyone had a problem with that they could join Jackson in his tiger cage for a friendly game of hide-the-salami.

I watched the media circus unfolding on the evening news, bewildered as hell and high as fuck, while Jackson sat behind the prosecutor's podium with a large, growling attack dog situated inches away from his terrified face.

When the US attorney brazenly overstepped the law to bag her "illegal terrorist alien," she failed to consider yet another hard fact: a law stating that 25,000 signatures petitioning for the review of a US attorney's reckless prosecutorial actions elicits mandatory congressional oversight, and this can potentially lead to the prosecutor's removal from office. And for that to happen, all it takes is a little publicity.

Upon learning about this law from my politically radical next-door neighbor Plotkin, I flew out to California, picked up a video camera, and hit the streets. Over the next several months, I conducted several hundred man-on-the-street interviews, focusing on a US attorney's office run amok. I also conducted several celebrity interviews, including Pepperpot, Noam Chomsky, and an unexpectedly passionate and angry Rosie O'Donnell. Then, with some help from an editor friend, I stitched together these interviews with archival footage from the Guantánamo press conference and a few news shows and sundry bits, and created a polemical documentary structured to touch the hearts and minds of enough clear-thinking citizens to force the review of the US attorney's "Jackson Action."

I sent the cut to the *The Daily Show* and crossed my fingers. Two days later, Jon Stewart introduced an edited version of my call-to-arms, and within three days my petition had swelled to over 250,000 signatures!

Several days later, with no explanation whatsoever from the US attorney's office, Jackson was transferred out of Guantánamo and sent to the LA County jail for possession of an undisclosed quantity of hashish. While no formal charges had ever been brought against Jackson for hash possession, and while the review of the US attorney's office as mandated by our ample signatures was never mounted, Jackson was back on American soil (albeit in prison), where due process plays a part in prosecutions, however minimally.

Jackson languished behind bars for the better part of a year while the dust settled and the government covered its tracks. Meanwhile, I continued to film Jackson's journey, and by the time Leona, Munsey, and I picked him up from jail, I was ready to rumble.

Three months later, *The Incarceration of Godfrey Jackson* was accepted to the Sundance Film Festival.

We arrived at the premiere in a half-ton pickup truck with Jackson tied to a stake, atop a bed of kindling, ready to be burned like a witch in Salem. The theater was packed and the screening ended in a several-minute standing ovation. As Jackson and I looked around the room at the cheering crowd, it became immediately clear to us that we'd finally achieved the goal we'd set out to achieve fifteen years prior: Jackson was back on the map and I was on it with him!

Trays of pot brownies were served at the premiere party. The Artist Formerly Known As Prince showed up to join in the celebration. People danced into the wee hours to the bumping beats of a live band. Robert Redford himself danced on the bar with a Native American chief, who gave me the nickname "Young Sunrise." It was the high point of my life—but it didn't last long.

FabFilms was quick to come to the table, intent on acquiring worldwide rights for a whopping six million dollars. But when I crunched the numbers, after taking into account the money I had already spent and how much I'd have to lay out to meet the distributor's delivery requirements, I'd owe *them* money! Jackson agreed with my reasoning; he'd spent his entire career getting bamboozled by the bean counters. The only problem was, my agent adamantly refused to negotiate our deal and simply wouldn't take no for an answer. On the last day of the festival, the deal I turned *down* was announced in all the trades. Everybody I'd ever known called to congratulate me for winning the jackpot and was subjected to my story about the corrupt realities of media distribution and accounting practices. But none of this ultimately mattered because Jackson and I were a unified front. We organized an impromptu press conference at the Salt Lake City airport, where we announced to the press and a random assemblage of UGG-booted film industry nitwits that we were going to show the next wave of independent filmmakers how to distribute a film without giving in to the corrupt Hollywood suits. We'd taken on the government and Hollywood was next!

Two months later, *The Incarceration of Godfrey Jackson* opened the intellectually rigorous True/False Film Fest in Columbia, Missouri. After our screening, we were scheduled to speak on a panel of legal scholars including Alan Dershowitz, Cornel West, and Camille Paglia about state vs. federal law in the drive to reform marijuana legislation. The show sold out immediately. But I sensed trouble. In the intervening weeks since our independent film distribution grandstanding at Sundance, Jackson's dedication to the master plan had begun to waver. For reasons I couldn't yet grasp, Leona and the ever-pugnacious Munsey had been lobbying violently against me.

I'd been waiting in the lobby of the Holiday Inn for two hours when Jackson finally arrived with a motley group of newly minted sycophantic fans in tow, clamoring for an autograph and the chance to take a picture with him. Afterward, he walked over and sat down next to me, slouching into the couch cushions.

This time, I remained upright, stiff-backed, bracing myself. He apologized for being late and said he'd been busy doing a radio interview with Leona about *his* film and had lost track of time. Then he casually reached into his beaded suede Navajo notebook organizer and extracted a legal document.

"Before I forget," he said, "Leona asked that you sign this before tonight's screening. Otherwise we won't be able to stick around for it."

I stared at the ten-page document he held out in front of me.

"It's just a formality," Jackson added, reaching back into his notebook and taking out a pen as I scanned page after page of legal jargon about copyrights and distribution rights all belonging to him and Leona.

"It looks like more than a formality to me," I responded. "It looks like you're asking me to assign you all rights to my film."

"Hey, mon, you did a great job. You made an amazing film. But it's time to let your baby go and move on. We've got important work to do on our next film. Let's let Leona take it from here." Jackson picked up the pen and held it out toward me. I stared back into his beady, bloodshot eyes. I'd always suspected there might be a killer behind the mask of goofy, pot-induced innocence and benevolent idiocy, but now I realized it wasn't about him being a killer and it wasn't about him being good or evil. After all was said and done, Godfrey Jackson wasn't the human embodiment of pot, he was the human embodiment of *pussy-whipped*.

Several weeks later, standing under the marquee of the Alamo Drafthouse in Austin, Texas, announcing the theatrical release of *The Incarceration of Godfrey Jackson*, a pleasant-looking man walked up to me and handed me an envelope. I opened it to read that I'd been served with a lawsuit. Jackson was claiming I had stolen the rights to his film and was demanding I give them back or pay him $500,000.

Even after the film's failed initial theatrical run and the serving of the lawsuit, I continued to shill for The Cause, telling the world after each screening and during countless radio interviews that Godfrey Jackson was comedy's equivalent to serious drama's Marlon Brando, martyred by the US attorney's office, a.k.a. the most onerous legal establishment since the Inquisition. All the while living through the unrelenting agony of an obstructionist lawsuit brought against me by the very person I'd fought on behalf of with unflinching love and loyalty. A bitter irony.

As the weeks wore on, my exhaustion intensified, and so with few options left and unable to defend myself in court any longer, I scraped together $10,000 to retain a bad-ass Hollywood litigator to step into the ring and brawl on my behalf. I felt a sudden swell of elation. Sure, I'd literally bought my way onto the corporate grid, which I despised, but maybe that's what it took to survive in a fundamentally corrupt legal justice system. Yet my momentary happiness dissolved when the lawyer realized I had no resources beyond my retainer to pursue a $100,000 litigation and steered me straight into a binding settlement. By the end of the day, I agreed to a term of three months to either raise the money to pay Jackson off or give him and his wife (and Munsey) the rights to the film I'd made in his defense.

With the clock ticking and on the verge of a total physical and mental collapse, I threw a Hail Mary into the end zone and called Jack Herer, a man famous for writing a book called *The Emperor Wears No Clothes*, about the history of hemp in America. The book reminds readers that the cover of every wagon that crossed the plains was made of hemp, that the *Mona Lisa* was painted on a canvas made of hemp, that the sails of the *Mayflower*, along with its ropes and riggings, were all made of hemp, that the Constitution of the United States was drafted on paper made of hemp fiber! In many respects, the hysteria that led to Godfrey Jackson being dubbed an enemy combatant and deported to Guantánamo was the same hysteria that had helped underwrite the prohibition of hemp.

When I was making *The Incarceration of Godfrey Jackson*, I had visited Jack Herer in the Florida Everglades to interview him, but at this point in his life, his sole interest was in the psychoactive fungus, *Amanita muscaria*. (Through a series of academic texts and clues from the Vatican, Herer had become convinced that Jesus Christ was a mushroom, as were Santa Claus and the prophet Mohammad.)

Calling Herer again was grasping at straws, but as it turned out, my hunch was right. The day after I reached out to him, he called me back with a very powerful lead.

Graham DeLorme was a Vietnam vet who, soon after coming back to the US from his third tour of duty, had discovered that the Federal Reserve was burning its old currency. Millions and millions in paper currency was going up in smoke every few weeks in incinerators, only to be replaced by crisp new government-issue bills. Upon learning this surreal detail about America's hair-raising banking system, DeLorme and several of his vet buddies from 'Nam had infiltrated the Federal Reserve's currency incinerators and, in the most clownishly simple heist of all time, made off with close to half a billion dollars in old bills without a trace.

I called DeLorme at his home on a private island in the Caribbean. He listened intently as I reeled out my tale of woe. He chuckled the whole time, and then, with no hesitation, offered to send me $500,000—some of those dirty bills—in a shoe box. It would be his pleasure, he said, to see a naïve idiot like me win the day after all the hell I'd been through for thinking I could actually alter a broken and corrupt world with a puff piece about an opportunistic comedian.

And then, just as suddenly, he said, "I've got a better idea. Why don't you move here with us? You can have a plot of land to build your own house with a view of the ocean and become a member of our small but growing utopian cooperative. Live off the grid, get laid, and frolic on the dunes where clothes are optional. The American judicial system is fucked and always will be. Maybe it's time to take your endless idealism and hope for a better world and focus it on growing organic tomatoes."

At the time, I was determined to get back on my corporate career path, not off it—*way* off of it—on some remote island in the Caribbean to live with a bunch of fruity utopian money launderers. And yet my *calculated risk* of choosing a life of creative self-direction and shortcuts to greatness hadn't panned out. And in addition to everything else I was dealing with, I'd received numerous death threats and more than one brick through my living room window, so taking DeLorme up on his random generous offer was a calculated risk as well.

After abandoning my film to Jackson, Leona, and Munsey, I never looked back. I had done my work and made my statement about our crazy government. Recently, a friend called to tell me Pepperpot and Jackson were reunited and touring the globe making millions of dollars, in part due to the film I'd made about Jackson's indictment, and I told him I was happy to hear it—but in truth, I couldn't have cared less.

As of this writing, I'm sitting on the deck of my small house, built with sustainable materials including bamboo and hemp. I just read the *New York Times* cover to cover with a bialy and a hot cup of coffee, while enjoying the view of the budding Lamb's Bread growing in my garden.

Bill Westmoreland

Edward M. Gómez is an art critic and historian, graphic designer, and environmental activist. He grew up in Morocco and Switzerland, and has lived and worked around the world. A former writer/correspondent at *TIME*, he has written for the *New York Times*, the *Japan Times* (Tokyo), *Reforma* (Mexico City), *Art in America*, *Art & Antiques*, *Metropolis*, *ARTnews*, *Raw Vision* (UK), and many other publications.

no smoking
by edward m. gómez

I.

I never smoked pot correctly.

Smoking pot never had an effect on me.

Sure, like many other kids in high school, I tried the occasional puff. However, compared to the high-volume consumption of the school's most devoted potheads-in-residence—theirs could have been measured in bushels, not ounces—my experiments with the legendary herb were, well, dopey at best. Laughable. Half-assed. Lame.

One time, having learned about my plight from one of the less-frequent but still avid tokers who, like me, was a straight-A nerd, one of the PIRs took it upon himself to come to my rescue and initiate me in the art and pleasures of reefer madness. But it was no go. Even that well-meaning tutorial failed, or I failed it. Either I did not inhale correctly or I did not hold enough of the holy smoke in my skinny frame long enough to feel its magic or I simply did not *believe*.

Perhaps that was it, for never before had I felt a need to escape from so-called reality, and even if I had, for me, this stinky stuff probably would not have been the ticket I would have chosen to take me where I wanted to go.

In fact, at school what I had wanted was to be able to penetrate and understand the "real" world more profoundly, with a richer sense of awareness than the average guy walking around in torn jeans and a rock-band T-shirt. I wanted to soar to new heights of consciousness and understanding, not be pulled down into the muck of pulse-stopping stoner bliss.

Maybe it was no accident that, while still in high school, during one of my routine prowls through a nearby college's library, I discovered the branch of philosophy known as phenomenology and the existentialist writings it had inspired, as well as Aldous Huxley's little book from 1954, *The Doors of Perception*, in which he described his experience taking mescaline, a hallucinogenic in the peyote cactus, which had been used for generations by indigenous peoples of the Americas. Still, although I found it fascinating to learn how certain chemicals could make a person view reality differently or even experience new, different realities, it was the one in which I was stuck that I still wished to inhabit—I still didn't have a license to drive around in it—albeit with more of the sense of unpredictable adventure that characterized the movements of Alice and her cohorts in Wonderland than with the passivity and resignation with which so many people around me seemed to slog through their days.

Had I walked into my chemistry class to find a gigantic egg perched on the edge of the lab table, reciting indecipherable verse, I would have wanted to know how it got there; by contrast, the PIRs would have found in such a vision an irresistible affirmation of pot love and a good reason to light up.

Time passed. I was many years older when I got high for the first time. It was in a garden in which a single, exemplary pot plant grew—in a tidy collection of horticultural gems, it was more of a scientific specimen than its owner's private, illicit indulgence—but even today I still don't know for sure whether or not it was the marijuana that got me high. Instead, there was something else that flourished in that oasis, something else that must have intoxicated me on a balmy summer night many years ago. It was some other kind of elixir, not a rare herb or a strange vegetable or the essential oil pressed from the leaf of some exotic shrub. Instead it was the wafting scent of a spirit, and that spirit was Claire's.

2.

High school, college, graduate school: I could not get enough of philosophy or art. In the past, having been the precocious kid who had covered the blackboard in "psychedelic" drawings when the class was out to lunch, I enjoyed nothing more than being left alone with my books to read for hours or with my colored pencils to create my own worlds on paper in long art-making sessions that stretched into the night. When I learned that skilled doodlers could make a living creating pictures for books and magazines, I focused my studies on that goal and became an illustrator.

For a while, after moving to New York, an artists' agency represented me and found me jobs; nowadays, on my own, I'm able to find enough work to support my cat and myself. That summer, in fact, I was very busy. I was working on a children's book and on a set of images of household appliances for a volume about twentieth-century inventions.

Then came the call. It was sometime during that very hot summer, and I was not expecting a new project to pop up.

"Hello, Eric? The illustrator?"

"Yes, this is Eric," I replied. The voice was that of an older woman, raspy and friendly at the same time. I asked: "Who's calling, please?"

"Oh, great. Glad I got you. I was leafing through some old magazines, and I came across your lovely illustrations. You have a charming style."

"Thanks," I said. "How did you track me down? How may I help you?"

"Well, I saw the name of an artists' agency in one of those magazines, a company that represents you, and I called them and—"

"Right. That was a few years ago," I interjected. "I'm on my own now."

"That's wonderful," the woman said. "Talented people deserve to succeed. I hope you're doing well. So, can you come over?"

"Uh, but you haven't told me who you are and what it is you're calling about," I said politely. "Are you looking for an illustrator for a publishing project?"

"Oh, I'm sorry. I'm Barbara—but everyone calls me Booba, although recently there's been something of a backlash, or maybe it's the heat—it's so hot!—and some people have started calling me Baboo—anyway, it should be Babs, right? Isn't Babs the nickname for Barbara?"

Barbara-Booba-Babs rattled on for a while before explaining that she lived in a town in the Hudson Valley, north of Manhattan. She and her husband would soon celebrate their thirty-fifth wedding anniversary. She wanted to commission some illustrations of her home as a gift for her husband.

"You mean pictures of your house?" I asked. I wanted to be sure my caller did not want portraits of herself and her husband, either separate pictures or a double portrait. I did not like making portraits, for I always became too psychological about it; I always ended up seeing too much and then capturing it too obviously—too much of the anxiety, insecurity, and indecision I felt emanating from any sitter. People always wanted attractive pictures of their clothes or hairstyles. I gave them X-ray-like portraits of their vulnerability instead.

"Well, yes, pictures of the house and the yard," Barbara-Babs said. "I don't have much of a garden. You can have the run of the place and find any spots you think might capture its spirit. That's the idea. I want to give Bob something special, a reminder of the home we've built together over—"

Suddenly B. went silent, as though responding to her own admonishment to stop rambling.

"Well," I said, "it's a bit of an unusual assignment. In effect, you're asking me to produce a portrait of your home."

"Exactly!" B. replied enthusiastically, her energy revived. "That's just what I'm looking for! Could you do it?"

As busy as I was with other work, I was not eager to take up a new assignment, but it sounded like a challenge, and, I admit, my caller intrigued me. It was clear that if I accepted the assignment, I would have to meet her in person.

We discussed a deadline and my proposed fee. We set a date for a rendezvous at her house, at which time I would meet B. and make some preliminary sketches of what I found there. Confirming our plans, I thanked her for her call and double-checked the directions she had given me.

"I'll make us a little snack; I'll have some refreshments ready," B. added before saying goodbye. "I love desserts."

3.

"Hi, there! Nice to meet ya. Let's smoke a joint!"

That was how Barbara-Booba-Babs greeted me when I showed up at her house in the late afternoon a few days after her phone call. In the scorching heat, I wore a nerd's summer uniform of khaki shorts, a white polo shirt, and new sneakers with white ankle socks. B. arrived at the door holding a big, round pitcher of lemonade in one hand. She appeared in a billowing pink kaftan printed with blue and white polka dots, and her hair—I could see some dyed-red blond strands peeking out—was wrapped in what appeared to be a dish towel masquerading as a turban. Her face was round, like the pitcher, pale and glowing, with neatly plucked brows that formed perfectly symmetrical arches above lively brown eyes. I could tell she was a thin woman under all that fabric. Before I could respond to her invitation, though, B. had grabbed my hand and pulled me firmly into the house.

"Take a look around," she ordered, "then head out back."

As she darted to the kitchen at the back of the house, I took in the content and character of Barbara and Bob's living room and dining room, and a short hallway that led to a staircase down to a lower floor. The house was built into the side of a hill, with its front yard and main entrance, where I had come in, on the upper level. Downstairs, I assumed, were the bedrooms. Out front I had noticed a gravel-covered driveway but no garage.

What I surveyed was a catalog of clutter, from 1960s Italian movie posters and large, animal-shaped sculptures of blown, colored glass to clear-plastic cubes at either end of a red-leather, club-room sofa and steel-framed armchairs with fuzzy, black-and-white-striped seats and backs. There was a cuckoo clock. There was a Mr. Peanut cookie jar. There were braided-macramé plant holders hanging from the ceiling with no flowerpots in their pockets; they held wine bottles instead. The dining room was packed with chairs—bar stools, bean bags, a Shaker straight-back, an antique rocker, an upholstered recliner—but no table at which to sit and eat a meal. An Oriental rug in the living room was old and faded; the green wall-to-wall shag carpet beneath it, which covered the entire upper floor of the house, was matted and needed to be raked—or ripped out and destroyed.

"Eric!" B. barked from the back of the house. "Come!"

I made my way through the kitchen to a screened-in porch overlooking, like a watchtower, a backyard dotted with a few large oak trees. The deep expanse of lawn appeared to be well-tended, and, catching my inquisitive gaze, B. explained: "That's Bob, my husband. He's good with grass. He takes care of the outside, and I take care of the inside—and Bob." For a moment B. looked sad. Then, as I sat down, she cheerfully poured me a glass of lemonade and added, with a wink, "And I'm good with grass too. Here, try this."

"What I was going to say before was, I've never been good at smoking pot," I offered sheepishly. "Maybe we should talk about the pictures you want and—"

"Huh? What's not to be good at?" my hostess retorted as she sucked on a joint the size of a carrot. "Here," she said, shoving it into my hand and wrapping my fingers around it. She lifted it to my lips and placed it in my mouth like a mother teaching an infant to lick its first lollipop. "Now, I'm gonna light this, and you're gonna breathe in and hold it—hold it till kingdom come, till the cows come home, till pigs start to fly. Just hold it!"

I wondered if watercolors, colored pencils, or my new set of colored felt-tip markers would be the best materials to use to capture, in art, the look and personality of Babs and Bob's home. I breathed in. I recognized the sweet burning-grass smell. I tried to hold the smoke in my lungs. I also lost track of the time and started coughing and gasping for air.

"That wasn't very good, Eric!" B. admonished. "Ya gotta do better than that in order to feel the effect."

I gulped my lemonade.

"Here, don't drink that. Drink this!" B. commanded, handing me a new glass, freshly poured from another pitcher that had been tucked away somewhere at her side. "This one has vodka. Drink up!" She watched me as, reluctantly, I guzzled the cool liquid like an obedient youngster drinking up all his milk.

"What are you looking at?" B. asked as she caught my eyes wandering across her backyard to her neighbor's. The next-door property was filled with neatly planted shrubs, young trees surrounded by deer-intimidating protectors, exuberantly colorful flower beds, and a very full-looking vegetable garden enclosed by a fence made of chicken wire and old tree branches.

"Come on," B. said, seizing my hand. "Let's take a walk around the house so you can see the outside." Pulling me down steep wooden stairs that led from the porch to the backyard, she led me around her house, back up to the front, where oak trees shaded the simple structure and big rocks surrounded untended flower beds. I made quick plain-pencil sketches in my notebook. B. sucked on the remains of the joint.

In the backyard again, we stood near the bottom of the stairs that led up to the screened-in porch. "I think I have it," I announced.

"What's that?" B. replied with a little cough. She pounded her chest with her fist.

"The views I'd like to paint to represent your home," I said.

"That's great, Eric! What do you have in mind?"

"Inside, the room with all the chairs—"

"Genius!" Babs declared. "I knew you were a real artist!"

"And outside, a view of the back of the house, looking up to the watchtower porch."

"I like the way you think, kid," B. cooed.

"But in order to get the right perspective, I'm going to have to set up my easel over there . . ." I pointed to a spot in her neighbor's backyard, near the enclosed vegetable garden.

"Oh, Eric," B. sighed, removing the remaining scrap of reefer from her lips and stashing it in the folds of her kaftan. "I don't know. That would mean asking that girl for permission to let you set up in her backyard, and I . . ."

"Well, unless your neighbor's really unfriendly, I'm sure she wouldn't mind allowing me to work there. It wouldn't take long."

B. looked at me and then glanced over at her neighbor's backyard. "Are you feeling *any* buzz from that joint?" she asked. "That was supposed to be pretty good stuff."

I replied that, unfortunately, I had not felt any notable effect. "Maybe next time," I said, adding: "So, what do you think? I could go next door and ask your neighbor for permission to set up my things in her yard and set a date for—"

"No, no, no, dear, we'll go together," B. replied, taking my arm and pulling me up the stairs to the back porch and into the kitchen. "But first let's get the lemonade—and we'll also bring the brownies."

4.

B. did not stand on ceremony when the time came to announce our arrival at her neighbor's home, even though, during the few seconds it took us to walk across her front yard to the house next door, she admitted that she had never even spoken with this person before; she had never even met her.

"Hi! I'm Barbara, but you can call me Booba or maybe Babs or whatever the heck else you might come up with, and this is Eric, and we're stopping by to say hello and ask if Eric might be allowed to stand in your backyard to paint a picture—of the back of my house, that is, not of your place; that would be an invasion of privacy, and I assure you that we're decent people and not into snooping or anything like that." B. managed to blurt out all of this before her neighbor, a woman who appeared to be a few years younger than myself, could even utter a word to welcome us. "Oh! And we brought a little snack. Very refreshing on a day like this. It's so hot."

"Well, hello. Nice to meet you," the younger woman replied. "I'm Claire. You live next door? Come in. Come in. You're right, it's hot. Don't stand there melting."

We stepped into a cool living room—there was no air-conditioning, but dark curtains were pulled shut to keep out the sun—outfitted with a large, oval-shaped rug and very little furniture. Near the center of the room lay four cats in various positions of repose.

"Let's go to the back porch," Claire said. "Here, let me carry that pitcher. I'll get some glasses."

"Thanks, dear. I'm delighted to meet you and also very embarrassed that I haven't made an effort to say hello before today."

"Oh, that's okay. I've been here awhile but mostly I've kept to myself," Claire responded, piquing B.'s curiosity.

"Why's that, dear? You're on the lam? Running from the law?" B. chuckled and added: "Just kidding, of course."

"No, nothing so dramatic," Claire said. "I had been working as a schoolteacher a few towns over, closer to the river . . ."

"The community college?" B. asked.

"No, an elementary school. Let's just say that I was getting tired of it, and I also had to undergo an operation . . ."

"Nothing serious?"

"Not really, just routine, but after that I wanted a change. So I looked around and I moved here. I wanted room for a vegetable garden."

"What do you do now?" I asked, anticipating B.'s next question.

"I copy-edit material for medical journals. Work at home. I'm not a doctor or a scientist but I'm good with technical language. I've copy-edited users' manuals for all kinds of appliances too. Really anonymous literary work, you could say."

We all laughed, and I mentioned that I was illustrating a book about modern inventions.

"Is that what you do?" Claire asked. "Barbara said something about painting."

"Yes, I'm an illustrator, and she has commissioned me to draw some pictures of her house . . ."

"For my husband, Bob, for our wedding anniversary; I thought it would be something different, you know," B. explained.

"I think that's a very original idea for an anniversary gift," Claire said. "You must be very attached to your home."

"Or to Bob," B. said reflexively.

"What do you all do?" Claire asked.

"Oh, I used to do this and that; I used to be a secretary at Bob's company, in fact. As for my husband, he's in gravel."

"Gravel?" Claire and I responded in unison.

"Yes. He owns a company that sells gravel for driveways, for private roads, for gardens."

"I suppose most people don't think much about gravel," I said.

"No, dear, it's not the sexiest subject. But hey, it bought us a house and all the junk that's in it, and here we are!"

Claire's screened-in back porch was smaller than B.'s. Because Claire's house was also built into the side of the same hill, its top floor overlooked the backyard from what felt like a high perch. She disappeared into her kitchen to fetch some glasses, plates, and a tray, and soon returned.

"Even though it's hot out there, would you like to see the garden?" she proposed. "In fact, there's a part of the vegetable garden that's covered. It's shady, and I think it would be fun to enjoy this snack together down there."

"Sounds good!" B. replied.

We placed the pitcher, brownies, and other items on the tray and left it on the lowest step of the staircase that led down to the backyard, then followed Claire as first she led us on a tour around the exterior of her house.

"Did you do all of the landscaping yourself?" I asked. "Did you make the flower bed walls?"

"Yes," Claire said. "I saved the branches I had cut down off the trees at the lower end of the yard and just started stacking them; I liked the way they looked and I like the way they've aged."

Around the house, everything looked as though it had very naturally sprung up on its own—flower beds, groups of flowering shrubs or young trees with very thin trunks—but Claire explained that she had carefully planned the layout of every inch of her garden.

"What's this gang over here?" B. asked as we made our way

around the far side of the house and returned to the backyard.

Claire told us that the shaded patch Barbara had noticed was filled with Christmas fern, maidenhair fern, lady fern, and Japanese painted fern.

"There really are so many kinds of fern? Who knew?" B. said, as she poked around in the pockets of her kaftan.

"Over there you have a butterfly bush, a beauty bush, and a spice bush," Claire pointed out, "and besides the big oaks—you have some too, Barbara—among the trees, there are some dogwoods, a white pine, and a Stewartia, which the Japanese call the 'summer camellia'; it's native to Korea and southern Japan. They have a beautiful flower."

"I think I noticed them earlier this summer," B. said as she bent down to pick up our refreshments. We all headed over to Claire's fenced-in vegetable and herb garden. As she had indicated, a light-colored tarp covered about a fourth of the large enclosure, casting shade over a patch of grass where nothing had been planted. We spread out there, on the ground. B. poured three glasses of lemonade, and Claire cut and served the brownies on small clear-glass plates.

"That's where I'd like to set up my easel to paint my picture of Babs's house," I said, pointing to a spot a few feet away from the far end of the enclosed garden.

"That's fine," Claire replied. "Whenever you want, just come and set up your things."

"Hey, everybody!" B. exclaimed. "Let's smoke some pot!"

"Huh?" Claire responded. "Really? I'm growing some, you know."

"What! Seriously?"

"Well, I decided to grow it just as a kind of experiment, just like I'm trying to grow tulsi, or holy basil—it's from India and used for tea—and wild bergamot and lemon verbena and apple mint. They're all used to make teas."

B. had fished out a little plastic bag of marijuana and some rolling papers from the depths of her kaftan and was busy rolling a joint as Claire described her plantings. As she spoke, she nibbled a brownie, stood up, and walked over to a tiny wooden table within the enclosed garden. She pulled open a drawer and removed a pair of gardening gloves, some tools, and a neatly folded white handkerchief, which she brought back and handed to B.

"Barbara," Claire asked, "what's in these brownies? Why do they taste like freshly mown grass?"

"That's because there's pot in them, dear," B. said. I choked on my own brownie as she divulged the secret of her recipe, which prompted B. to look at me and remark: "So, Eric, if smoking it doesn't work for you, maybe eating it will."

"Here, Barbara, you can have this," Claire said, handing B. the folded cloth. "I removed the stems and dried the leaves myself. But I warn you, I know nothing about cultivating pot. That's my lone plant right there." We all glanced over at what appeared to be a healthy marijuana plant growing tall among the other vegetables and herbs. Then Claire looked at me and asked, "What does she mean, smoking pot doesn't affect you? Have you tried many times?"

"No. I mean, I'm not a pothead or anything . . ."

"I am," B. weighed in from the side as she unfolded Claire's handkerchief, found a fluffy pile of dried leaves inside, and began to roll a second joint.

"It's not as though I'm always trying to get high," I added.

"I am," B. chimed in as she labored.

"Well, I hardly ever smoke pot either," Claire explained. "I really don't know why I planted it this year. Like I said, it's just an experiment."

B. knocked back the last of her drink and poured herself a second glass. As I had expected, she had brought the spiked lemonade with us to Claire's place. My head began to spin.

Holding up the two joints, B. declared: "Okay, kids. We're going to do a taste test and we're going to get Eric high."

5.

There are times in life when the best thing to do, perhaps the only thing to do, is to throw dumb hesitation to the wind—to strike back hard at the underlying fear that fuels it—and peel off all your clothes and jump in the pool while everybody is watching, or hold your nose and take a bite of the escargots in garlic sauce that look like twice-boiled pencil erasers, or dare to place a kiss on a pair of lips that, until or unless you do, will never know the urgency of your desire. There are times when resistance to whatever may be calling is futile.

So it was that I allowed B. to place the first of her freshly prepared joints between my lips. Claire watched and reached for her drink. "Barbara, what's in this lemonade?" she asked.

"Mama's special recipe," B. replied as she massaged my shoulders. I was sitting up, with my legs stretched out in front of me. "Now, Eric, I already lit that joint and got it started. I'm gonna light it again, and you're gonna breathe in and hold it, then slowly release the smoke. That's the idea."

Mama slid forward to face me and lit the joint. I tried to follow her instructions. Claire observed me with a serious look. At that moment I assumed that, until recently, when she had worked as a schoolteacher in a nearby town, she must have been a science teacher—and probably a very good one.

I exhaled.

"Again!" B. commanded. I thought the taste of the just-smoked pot had been somewhat muted by the strong, lingering taste of the pot brownie I had just finished eating. "This time take a puff of Claire's blend."

"Claire's blend?" Claire asked.

"Actually, it's not a blend. It's one hundred percent your pot," B. said. "Here we go."

I took the second joint and repeated the inhale-exhale routine. "May I have a sip of lemonade," I asked my examiners.

"It's like a taste test of the finest wines!" B. noted. "Now he wants to cleanse his palate."

Claire handed me a glass. I took a gulp and managed to eliminate some of the strong, overlapping tastes in my mouth. I felt dizzy.

"Give him some time," B. instructed. "Relax, Eric. Let me know when you're ready for more." Then she puffed on each joint, one after the other, performing a taste test of her own. Taking a break from her indulgence, she said, "Oh, Claire! I'm sorry, I completely forgot about *you*. Would you like . . . ?"

"No, that's okay. You enjoy it. I'm fine."

By now I had spread out and was lying on my back. The sun had begun its lazy descent. Claire lay on her back next to me, to my right. B. sat in a shapeless lump to Claire's right, still savoring the first joint, then the second. Time passed. A gentle breeze rustled the deep green leaves of the Japanese Stewartia.

B. interrupted the silence. Softly, she said, "You know, Claire, if you ever need any gravel, just give us a shout. Bob would be glad to give you all you want—I mean free of charge."

"Well, thank you. That's very nice of you to offer—"

"With pleasure! It's the least a good neighbor can do. And that goes for you too, Eric. Free gravel. As much as you want—although I guess you don't have a big need for gravel where you live."

I grunted. I was not sure if I was high from the pot or tipsy from B.'s spiked lemonade or simply enervated and even nauseous from the heat. The brownie had not helped. Would I ever know what it felt like to get high from smoking pot? Was *this* it, in some perverted, upside-down, Eric in Wonderland kind of way?

The kaftan at Claire's side was spread out, with B. in it, flat on the ground, gazing up at the sky. One of Claire's cats, a big tabby, entered the garden, knocked over a lemonade glass with its swinging tail, and brushed up against B.'s thigh before settling down there, in a thicket of polka dots. The moon had arrived in the early-evening sky.

I wondered how holy basil had earned its name. For the Indians, was it a sacred plant? I thought about how interesting it would be to make drawings of all of the plants in Claire's garden. First I would have to do some serious research. I remembered that the best botanical illustrations always included each plant's distinctive details. I wondered if watercolors, colored pencils, or my new set of colored felt-tip markers would be the best materials to use to capture the spirit of Claire's garden and all that was in it. I thought that, with a few pounds of very small gravel neatly spread out in a shallow tray, I could create a miniature version of one of those Japanese Buddhist-temple gardens, the kind in which some dutiful monk, probably pulled away from his most profound meditations, must attentively rake the finely crushed stones that are symbols, in their smallness, silence, and durability, of the ocean's countless waves or the timelessness of time or the notion that an entire universe can be found in even the tiniest grain of sand. I wondered if Bob was a good man and if, over the years, he had personally chosen all those chairs. Who had picked out the cuckoo clock? A second cat approached and snuggled in, between my feet.

"Am I high? Did I get high?" I asked, addressing my question to no one in particular.

"Do you feel high?" B. replied.

"I don't know. I mean, maybe. Or, well, I really can't say."

"You're high," B. asserted. "I'd say that one of the two pot specimens had some effect. But then again . . ."

"Only you would know, Eric," Claire said, turning her head slowly to face me. "You would know."

"By the way, dear," B. offered, "*your* pot is much better than *my* pot. The results of the taste test are in. You win. It's that green thumb."

Looking up, I couldn't believe it—I could clearly see the Big Dipper and some other constellations whose names I should have known but could not recall. "Wow! You can't see any of this down in the city. The city lights wash out everything." Even the crusty, textured surface of the moon was vaguely visible. "I'm sorry I was such a failure at getting high," I said to my companions as another cat climbed up and settled down, in a sphinx position, with its front paws turned in, on my chest, facing me.

"You're no failure," Claire consoled, as she took my right hand in hers and, on her right side, found B.'s hand floating above her kaftan and gave it a squeeze. We lay there in silence for a long time, with two cats purring, and cicadas buzzing in the bushes. The sky sparkled, and the moon glowed.

"There are many ways to get that feeling of being high, you know," Claire said, peering into the night's vast ocean of unfathomably far-away, intoxicating eternal light. Taking my hand in hers and lifting it up above our heads like a teacher's pointer as we lay there on the grass, she turned to me and whispered, as though revealing a long-kept secret known only to the members of an ancient tribe: "All you really have to do, if you're looking for it on a night like this, is lie back, look up, reach up, and touch the stars."

PART IV

GOOD & BAD MEDICINE

Raymond Mungo is the author of *Famous Long Ago, Total Loss Farm, Palm Springs Babylon,* and many other books. An original founder of Liberation News Service in Washington, DC in 1967, he has published articles on the 1960s counterculture in periodicals and anthologies. *Famous Long Ago* was recently reissued in paperback as a college textbook in American history. Mungo lives in Southern California, where he is also a social worker tending primarily to AIDS patients and the severely mentally ill.

kush city
by raymond mungo

GOT KUSH? screamed the green billboard adorned with a sparkling crystallized bud, Humboldt quality, looming over Pacific Coast Highway and Cherry Avenue in Long Beach, California, a thousand miles south of grass country. A bold black 1-800 number was prominently advertised. That was it, no explanation, a freaking ad for reefer, as big as the Ritz. I damn near crashed the Honda hatchback into the car ahead of me. The nation was swirling down the 2008 rabbit hole of depression, panic was in the air, and some old Republican Vietnam War POW who thought marijuana was a gateway drug to heroin was running for president. But this cheerful note lifted my spirits.

I had plenty of pot, but no "kush." Smoking grass daily since 1963, I used it as a tool for writing, but in fifty years of herbal appreciation never called it kush, and the stuff I got from Charlie was definitely *not* in that exalted category. Charlie home-delivered rather ordinary shit, but he was reliable, affordable, and always ready. As a fifty-five-year-old sometime jazz musician, he needed the extra green, but he sold the brown. Charlie carried only one variety at a time. The price never changed, but if he thought something was extraordinary, he'd recommend buying ahead. He dispensed professionally sealed packets for fifty bucks. No dickering, no discounts, no scales. Looked like a quarter, but he called it a lid.

Charlie was a nice guy, and I was glad to be free of the lifelong pursuit of fickle dealers, hanging around squalid apartments waiting for delivery, now that I'm an old fart. If the neighbors thought anything of the gray ponytailed beatnik visitor who showed up with some regularity but never stayed more than five minutes, they didn't comment on it. The pungent aroma of the Mexican rag weed seeped from my front door into the hallway, but I wasn't the only head in the building. The evangelical Christian on the floor below, who began and ended every conversation with invocations to the deity, more or less smoked all day long and never seemed to go to work. He drove a silver Beemer and had a trophy girlfriend.

"Hey, Charlie, what's with all these *GOT KUSH?* billboards popping up everywhere around town?" I ventured.

He just groaned. "It's driving me out of business, man. All my best customers in Silver Lake have gone legal." He lived in LA.

"Legal?" What a concept.

"As in medical. You know, with a doctor's prescription. The dispensaries are everywhere now."

"They are?" I hadn't noticed a single one in Long Beach, and anyway, who ever heard of a pot dispensary? "But that's only for people with AIDS or cancer or some other horrible disease."

"Nah, man, anybody can get a prescription. You can claim insomnia, migraines, appetite problems, mental stuff, anything, man. You pay the doctor's fee and you get the prescription. Nobody gets turned down."

Holy kush. Charlie was either giving our friendship a higher value than his business acumen, or had figured that my loyalty to him would dissuade me from trying this legal maneuver. Probably the latter, although in fact I was just a customer, not particularly a close friend. I was already scheming to get some of this stuff. What did I have to lose? The doctor might find me too goddamn healthy to qualify.

"Mental stuff" reminded me that I had vials of antidepressants and anxiety pills with my name on them, prescribed by my regular physician at the HMO. Never mind that both vials were badly outdated. Mental illness had been documented. I used the antidepressants exactly one day, then ditched 'em because they gave me a *strong* desire to kill myself. The doc offered to replace them with some other kind of antidepressant but I said, no, I'd rather be a little depressed than suicidal. The anxiety pills came in handy during a six-month stint in France, where pot was hard to find, and they actually helped me tolerate the dreaded cannabinoid withdrawal syndrome, which every daily user knows sets in after ten days of abstinence. The French smoke hash mixed with black tobacco and cured with some kind of poison that always makes me choke.

Coughing is one thing, and actually considered a good sign, but choking is another.

I set up an appointment with the pot doctor at a Medi-Cann clinic on a seedy block of Atlantic Avenue. It cost $110 for the visit, discounted if you happened to be on Medicare or Medicaid, and the operator explained that it was only sixty-five dollars for the annual renewal thereafter. Cash or credit cards were accepted, no checks.

Medi-Cann was a storefront with dirty windows covered by closed Venetian blinds on a block of abandoned retail locations—the only other functioning business, a corner liquor store. The tiny sign on the door gave no indication of the nature of the place, which was hard to find and would have attracted little notice except for the scaggy-looking long-haired young guys smoking cigarettes right outside. I arrived fifteen minutes before the clinic started seeing patients, but the place was already packed, only one forlorn folding chair unoccupied.

The Mayo Clinic this was not, but it might be the *Mungo* Clinic. Unlike any doctor's office I'd ever seen, it had no magazines or medical brochures, but rather stacks of advertisements for Long Beach pot dispensaries and specialty marijuana publications, mostly from Northern California, with dispensary advertising from all over the state. Postcards touted twenty percent discounts for new patients, "free" joints, pipes, grams of hash, and rolling papers with a minimum "donation" and "membership." I crammed a bunch of these into my briefcase and sat down with a Julian Barnes novel from the library.

All the patients in the waiting room were strapping young men in their late teens or early twenties, Testosterone City, except for one old guy in a wheelchair, very talkative, who seemed like a Vietnam vet/panhandler, and an old woman missing front teeth. Of course, you can't tell just by looking at someone what his or her particular ailment may be, but this roomful of youths could not *all* be suffering from terminal illness. They joked around loudly, a party going on.

Every five or ten minutes, a young woman in capri pants opened the door to the inner office and called a new patient by name. The nurse or medical assistant, I guessed. Given the number of people crammed in the room and the frequency of her appearances, I assumed there must have been three or four doctors on duty. Nonetheless, by the time I was summoned, it was forty-five minutes past my scheduled appointment. These docs were evidently on Kush Daylight Time.

When the young woman summoned me into the back room, I was startled to find that she was the doctor—Dr. Monica. No nurse, assistant, or other physician was on duty. The office was devoid of trappings associated with medical practice, she never took my blood pressure or weighed me, there wasn't a stethoscope or even a computer terminal in sight. The room was furnished with a battered wooden desk covered with stacks of files, on which a gooseneck lamp was clamped, and folding chairs for doctor and patient. I produced the vials of outdated pills, which she scrutinized briefly, nodded, and hastily scrawled notes on what seemed to be my chart, but made no comment. She asked only how often I smoked pot, and how—joint, pipe, vaporizer? Every day, for over forty-five years, usually in joints.

"You ought to give yourself a vacation from it for a week or ten days every now and then, give your lungs a break. You'll also get more value for your money when you do go back to it."

(Fair enough, I thought, but in fact not gonna happen.) (Except in France.)

"And you should look into a vaporizer. Some daily smokers can't make the transition, but the advantage is that it delivers the THC without the harsh smoke. The best one is from Vape Brothers." (Now *there's* an idea.)

Thank you, doctor ma'am. She marched me back to the receptionist who'd taken my $110 and handed me a document certifying my prescription for twelve months. The secretary took a Polaroid photo and promised I'd get a laminated ID card in the mail within two weeks. The prescription was ready for immediate use, and the nearest dispensary was only a few blocks away.

Natural Health Collective, identified only as NHC on the door, was in an alley behind a commercial building, up an outdoor wooden staircase to the second floor. Even with the street address from its postcard advertisement, the place was clandestine, the door locked. A handmade sign advised me to *Ring Buzzer for Admittance*. I noticed a video camera mounted above me and a wave of paranoia washed over me. The door clicked and I entered a small waiting room with a cashier shielded behind what looked like bullet-proof glass.

"Your first time?" the guy asked.

"Yeah."

"Can I see your doctor's rec and driver's license or photo ID?"

I slid the documents through the narrow glass slot.

"Have a seat, this will just take a few minutes," he said.

Voices murmured behind the wall and another locked door

under video surveillance. Ten minutes passed while I wondered what was going on and felt vaguely insecure about the clerk having my driver's license and doctor's prescription, but he emerged smiling from his cage and returned my belongings to me.

"You're clear." A buzzer sounded and he waved me to the entrance of the inner sanctum. "One for the showroom," he barked into a walkie-talkie contraption as the door swung open.

It was a pot smoker's candy store. Glass display cases held rows of Mason jars crammed with gorgeous buds labeled with fanciful names. *Purple Haze. Strawberry Cough. Blue Dream. Jedi OG. Super Sour Kush.* Sensitive electronic scales and boxed displays of paraphernalia covered the glass countertops. One wall was dominated by a huge white board on which varieties and prices were posted in erasable felt tip. Prices were quoted by gram, eighth, or full ounce and got higher with perceived quality and more economical with greater volume, but my first impression was pure sticker shock. The cost was more or less double Charlie's. As a first-time patient, I would get a twenty percent discount as well as some freebie—choice of a free gram or joint with minimum of purchase of an eighth, choice of a small pipe, pack of papers, or lighter.

All the clerks were scantily clad young women showing considerable décolletage, grinning broadly. They jabbered away, gaily advising me about the special deals, like extra-heavy eighths on Tuesdays, free eighths in exchange for referring a new patient, and a ten percent discount for seniors and the disabled. I qualified for the former, but you couldn't combine it with a first-timer discount. Payment was by cash only, no plastic, checks, or receipts. The weed was bagged in the familiar mortar-and-pestle prescription sack used by regular pharmacies.

The product was outstanding, like the best Maui Wowee, and I was instantly too spoiled to get off on Charlie's stuff anymore.

Since every dispensary offered the twenty percent introductory discount plus "free gift," I became a first-time patient in each.

With new dispensaries popping up all over town, they soon outnumbered Starbucks. My newbie status lasted a good two years before I had to visit the same one twice. Each had its unique properties, some larger than others, but all of them were fairly hard to see from the street, marked only by initials. The prices were remarkably competitive with one another, almost universal, as was the cash-only/no-receipt payment policy. The quality varied, but I was seldom disappointed. A few of these shops were evidently not playing by the rules. I saw a tall, golden Adonis in tank top and shorts buying three thousand dollars' worth of bud—there was no specific dosage on the prescription, but the medicine was by law for personal use only—who remarked casually that he was "buying for my collective in Huntington Beach." One sleazy outfit offered sample hits from a vaporizer on-site, *not* kosher, and one proprietor boasted of a full guarantee: "If you're not satisfied, bring it back and I'll replace it," he crowed. One place actually had a bubble gum machine in its lobby and permitted children to wait there while their parents shopped the showroom. An elderly retired nurse from Orange County ran her own tiny shop, called the Green Nurse, and offered to weigh you and take your blood pressure. A young, bearded stoner guy in torn jeans took the money and put it in his pocket before handing you your purchase.

I finally settled on Quality Discount Caregivers (QDC), one of the busiest dispensaries in town, which had a huge selection of top-grade stuff. The prices weren't any lower but they featured a kind of "frequent flyer" program. Save the empty plastic vials from twelve eighths, then redeem them for a free one, a baker's dozen. Zig-Zag papers were gratis. On the fifteenth of the month, everything in the store was twenty-five percent off, and patients lined up on the sidewalk, but even on regular days you always had to wait your turn to get into the vault. The clerks were all mostly bosomy, half-naked chicks, the patients almost all male. I wondered how they got away with hiring only the youngest and most endowed female clerks—wasn't that a violation of equal opportunity employment or something? The amount of money changing hands was staggering. Security precautions were practically military, with TV monitors everywhere and muscular, young, uniformed security guards with "badges" and guns.

By 2010, Long Beach had become a kushier town than Amsterdam, Bangkok, Maui, Bern, or Lugano. All those places had anti-marijuana laws they simply declined to enforce. Of course the brown cafés of Amsterdam were the most famous, the novelty of being able to walk into a storefront and score your stash over the counter almost unique in the world. But Switzerland, quietly and without controversy, has a similar system—in fact, growing and possessing marijuana has never been against Swiss law, but they cleverly get around it with a loophole; they call it hemp and prohibit its use "for narcotic purposes." Hah hah hah.

The difference in California is that the storefront dispensaries are legal under state law. The state passed the first medical marijuana initiative in the nation, the famous Proposition 215, way back in '96, and many attempts to repeal it have been soundly rejected by the electorate. Federal law adamantly forbids pot, but when Obama took office, he very early indicated that his attorney general would not pursue medical marijuana patients. Cities and towns in California adopted their own local ordinances, adding to the confusing miasma of different laws.

How groovy is that? But some upscale towns and better neighborhoods shunned the dispensaries. I found myself in places I wouldn't frequent after dark. I raced past loitering bums eyeballing every customer who emerged from the store. I parked in conspicuous spots.

While few people would deny medicine to patients with serious illnesses, everyone knew you could get a prescription for nothing worse than a headache, and public objections to blatantly obvious pot stores grew into an uproar. Parents complained about cannabis storefronts located near schools and parks. Neighbors took offense at the late-night shenanigans and clusters of loitering stoners on the street. The Long Beach City Council dickered over the matter, divided into liberals and conservatives like the Supreme Court, and finally crafted a "compromise"—a bizarre lottery system intended to award a limited number of dispensary licenses and thus rein in the explosive growth of the industry. Some rogue dispensaries ignored it entirely and kept opening their doors and raking in cash until the city cops raided and smashed up their shops. A full-scale war was underway by 2011.

Uh-oh. Trouble in Paradise. But every time I asked one of the babes if the dispensary was going to be closed down, she said something like, "Oh, no, it's all just politics, it's all about money, we're staying open, here you go honey, see you next time!"

Eventually the city got the amount of stores down to what it considered a manageable number, but then the federal government filed suit to invalidate the local ordinance, ruling that city law could not supersede federal. The crackdown seemed to contradict Obama's original promise not to interfere with medical users, and was applied selectively to a few places that were singled out. Total chaos descended by the summer of 2012, with dispensaries vowing to defy the ban and pushing for a popular vote. Medical marijuana doesn't fail at the ballot box.

This unstable, troubled paradise could not survive indefinitely and after six more months of feverish wrangling, Long Beach closed down its pot shops in August 2012, while LA did the same. Anticipating this tragedy, I'd stocked up in advance. In the last couple of weeks, the store was crammed from opening to closing. I saw all my street buddies. Everyone was worried sick. But we joked about it and the girls winked. I knew the end was near, however, when on my last visit there was only one babe on duty, the others having been replaced by grim-looking hairy men, the bosses.

Not every store complied, of course, but the rogue operations seemed doomed to violent police raids.

Sob. The *GOT KUSH?* billboards are gone now and it appears that the golden era of freewheeling liberation is behind us, but the horse got out of the barn and won't go back. I shopped at one of the several dispensaries who refused to shut, and they were welcoming new customers by the score with a twenty-five percent discount. The scene there resembled rush hour on the freeway, with slow-moving lanes of potheads.

Even the owners forced to shut down now make the dubious claim that they can still deliver kush to your home quite legally as long as you have the doctor's letter, and certainly these home deliveries will be more difficult to regulate than public stores, since they are essentially invisible. There's no risk of running out of medicine.

But in five years it's come full circle in Kush City. I wonder if Charlie has branched into the "legal" home delivery business. I wish I hadn't lost his number. But the babe slipped hers into the bag.

Marion Ettlinger

RACHEL SHTEIR is the author of three nonfiction books, most recently *The Steal: A Cultural History of Shoplifting*. She has written for many magazines and newspapers, including the *New York Times* and the *New Republic*. During the 2011 Chicago mayoral election, she wrote a weekly column for *Tablet* magazine about Rahm Emanuel called "The Rahm Report." She is the recipient of many awards for her writing, and has taught at many universities.

julie falco goes west: illinois poster girl for legalizing medicinal cannabis leaves town

by rachel shteir

I first met Julie Falco in September of 2012, after she had decided to go to California. I was looking for a person involved in the fight to make medical marijuana legal in Illinois. Everyone mentioned Julie.

When she greets me at the door of her nearly bare one-bedroom apartment, one of the first stories she tells me is how three years ago, she flew to DC to attend the Marijuana Policy Project's fifteenth-anniversary gala—fifteen states in fifteen years. The event was held at the Hyatt Regency on Capitol Hill. The MPP was honoring her, Cheech and Chong—who received a Trailblazer Award—and Joseph McSherry, a physician who helped pass medical marijuana laws in Vermont.

Julie is telling me this because despite her efforts, and the efforts of many others, IL House Bill 30, which would make medical marijuana legal in Illinois, has yet to pass. Julie herself is less active in the movement than she used to be, but she remains the best-known patient advocate in the state, a rock star of the movement, albeit one who often had to sleep on the floor of the hotel room because the beds were too soft for someone with multiple sclerosis.

Recalling that night, Julie says she didn't know three hundred people would show up at the MPP gala to support her.

Nor did she plan to bring up one of her biggest irritations—the word "marijuana," or as she sometimes says, "the M word"—which she stopped using around 2005 when she concluded that it prevented legislators from taking the plant's medicinal uses seriously. Since then, she has always "thought in cannabinoid." When she took the podium that night in DC to give her speech, the plea for changing the word to cannabis just tumbled out. Later, she was gratified to see Tommy Chong agree that the government uses the word marijuana to demonize pot. It was a golden evening and Julie could not have imagined that six months later, her dedication to cannabinoid science would take another shape—that she would begin to dream of California.

Today, pursuing that dream is how Julie spends most of her time. She is forty-seven, but she could be mistaken for ten years younger despite needing a walker to move around inside her apartment. She has an open, unlined face, brown hair, and brown eyes. The day I visit, she is wearing a peach-colored T-shirt with sequins splattered around the front, light-colored jeans, and a thin silver ring on her thumb. She arranges her hair in the style of Dorothy Hamill and is quick to smile.

Julie has had MS since 1986 when she was a communications major at Illinois State University in Normal, 133 miles from Chicago, and a girl guitarist in an alternative rock band, which went by various names but ended up as Zero Balance. Home for spring break to attend her mother's second wedding, she first noticed her foot dragging in the supermarket parking lot. Before she had time to worry about the foot, it cleared up. She went back to school.

Two years later, Julie relapsed with totally different symptoms. Now she couldn't see. The disease "hit her optic nerve." There was no cure. She was told to go home and rest. Instead, she tried to live her life. She got a job at Design Lab Chicago, a theatrical lighting firm, and then went to Europe for a month. She backpacked, limping through France and Switzerland. She stayed with her grandfather's sister in Germany in his 500-year-old house. She went to Amsterdam, she says, although she does not elaborate on the obvious—the legality of marijuana in Holland. From that time until 2004, she tried maybe forty different treatments—acupuncture, hydrotherapy, Zanaflex, Valium, BETASERON. She was "debilitated, lethargic, one big ball of symptoms." She walked with a cane, and then two canes, and then a walker. (Now she uses her walker indoors and outdoors a power scooter or a wheelchair.)

Julie was scared. She had many different symptoms, including facial paralysis. She moved back to Chicago. She wanted to be near her family and moved into a small apartment on the second floor, above her grandmother's, in Beverly, on Chicago's South Side.

Twenty-six years later, Julie is tired. No one understands her dedication to cannabis, not even her mother, who told her she understands that it is her only medicine but that she hopes Julie keeps an open mind. What about Big Pharma, why don't they keep an open mind? Julie asked.

She is tired of reading about drugs that suppress symptoms. She wishes for a drug that will eliminate symptoms. Most of the new ones are focused on newly diagnosed people, she complains. And when you read the side effects, when you get down to risk of death, "Let's eliminate that one right off the bat," she jokes. She is often joking.

These days when Julie wants to leave the apartment, which she does no more than ten times a month, she has to call the fire department. She could have built a ramp but ultimately decided against it. She now lives on the first floor in a typical one-bedroom on the northside, a little down at the heels, probably built in the 1930s, with a fake fireplace. There is a large massage table folded up in its cover by one wall and boxes piled by the window. She has been in this apartment for over twenty years. So, when she recently donated, gave away, and threw out around eighty percent of her possessions, it was a big job.

Now, every day Julie spends around four or five hours working on leaving town, to move to Berkeley or Oakland. It's hard to find an accessible, affordable apartment. She was going to go with a friend but that person got ill. She's exploring hiring a personal assistant. She's on a waiting list for six or eight apartments.

"I'm not completely clear on my exit strategy. No one has responded to me. Is anyone interested that I'm giving my body to cannabinoid science?"

When I ask about cannabinoid, Julie is happy to explain: "Cannabinoid science is not marijuana. It's a common mistake. Anyone who uses the word marijuana, they are living under Prohibition to demonize this plant. I use the words cannabis and cannabinoid medicine. I am studying the science. This is what the plant is called; there are cannabinoids; we have a cannabinoid system in our bodies, even if you do not imbibe in the cannabis system. I've written a book, it took me five years to research: *The Cannabis Papers: a citizen's guide to cannabinoids*. It's on Amazon and on lulu.com. It's a signaling system, it regulates all the other systems of your body. We are deficient in this system."

From 2004 until 2011, when Julie worked to advocate legislation allowing medical marijuana in Illinois—today seventeen states have these laws but Illinois still isn't one of them—she would drive the several hours to Springfield about once a month. Then, in July 2010, she was invited to speak at the Science and Compassionate

Care Seminar at the Radisson Plaza Hotel in Kalamazoo, Michigan. Also invited were Dr. William L. Courtney and his wife Kristen Peskuski, who had managed to control lupus and many other ailments by juicing cannabinoids. Kristen talked about how cannabinoids can best be absorbed into the body by juicing, putting maybe ten or fifteen fresh palm-sized leaves in a blender with some apples or some carrots, and drinking the mixture like a smoothie, daily. "The focus is always on smoking the biggest, grandest bud; there's gotta be a paradigm shift, because the juicing is what cures you."

And juicing was best accomplished in California.

Julie's tiny, old-fashioned Chicago kitchen doubles as her war room and she keeps manila folders full of clippings in piles. She hands me a printout of a multicolored pie chart showing the amount of CBD (cannabidiol)—one of the compounds in the cannabis plant—and the amount of THC (tetrahydrocannabinol), which she says is less able to heal disease. On the chart, dozens of arrows point outward, each representing its own compound with its own healing properties.

Julie started taking cannabis in 2004, when she had already been ill for nearly twenty years. She was so ill she was thinking of suicide. A lot of things contributed toward her decision to try using cannabis as a treatment for MS: she had smoked in college, and while researching online she read about a woman with glaucoma who used it. At the same time, she began talking to Illinois NORML (National Organization to Reform Marijuana Laws).

Soon Julie began baking one-inch cube brownies and eating them three times a day. It helped with her symptoms and she thought, *This is fantastic*. She could speed around the living room doing twenty to thirty laps, exponentially increasing her energy level.

Each pan of brownies contained about half an ounce (roughly fourteen grams) of marijuana. According to Illinois law, possessing ten to thirty grams of pot is a misdemeanor with a maximum penalty of a year in prison and a $2,500 fine. Julie tried not to think about that. But cannabis helped so much that her most immediate response was gratitude. The sensation wasn't like smoking where the effect goes to the brain. She was on an even keel all day long and it kept her numbness and tingling at bay so she could function well. Gradually, she weaned herself off pharmaceuticals and now she only takes Tylenol with codeine.

Julie began with a brownie mix, mostly Duncan Hines Double Fudge. She moved on to Ghirardelli brownie mix. She refined the recipe, sautéing what she genteelly calls "the plant material" in olive oil to release the benefits in it and to evenly distribute it. In other words, so she wouldn't choke on a clump. She included many "add-ins," such as walnuts and hemp seeds. More recently, though, she switched to what the NORML website calls Ginger Snap Surprise, which she buys already made, because she is too tired to bake.

Julie "takes" cannabis in a tincture of glycerine from an old brown glass bottle with an eyedropper, which goes right into her bloodstream. The tincture can also be made with flavored alcohol or with Everclear. There is also cannabis honey, the heat of which, stirred into tea, helps protect the compounds.

She likes dark chocolate and there is a box of chocolate almonds on the kitchen table. She takes her hemp juice, hemp oil. Sometimes she stops the cookies and brownies, like you would any medication. She is concerned about titration—in other words, how much medicine is good for her body.

Even back when she was "taking" brownies, Julie was sure that the changes she was going through were too profound to keep to herself. She began to speak about cannabis publicly and testified before the Illinois Senate, which, at that time, was in the first year of hearing a bill to legalize medical marijuana. Right away she wondered whether she should use her real name: She thought, *Wow, do I say I'm Julie F. or Julie Anonymous? I'm talking about all my stuff and something that's illegal. I can't imagine sitting in a jail cell.*

Then Julie read an article in the *Washington Post* about Jonathan Magbie, a paraplegic arrested for marijuana possession, who wound up in a cell where he couldn't communicate with the guards.

"They found him dead, soaked in his own urine," Julie says. "Are you kidding me? This is what we're coming to? Someone who doesn't have fully functioning limbs can't take something that helps him? It's just insanity. Well, I have use of my limbs, I have use of my voice. I am Julie Falco and it makes me feel better."

Julie began to visit every legislator in Springfield, making trips once or twice a month to tell her story, which back then not a lot of people were doing. Still, in the ensuing six years, as state after state passed laws legalizing marijuana for medical use, Illinois did not. The Marijuana Policy Project would set up a hotel room and transportation, and she would pretty much have to pack it up, spend a few days down there, bring her wheelchair, going through every office in the capital. It was taxing—she would get tremors just from the noise and the crowd, her nerves were so sensitive she couldn't process it all. It got easier over time. She'd bring a little container of brownies or ginger snap cannabis cookies. She would pull them out and say, "This is my medicine."

Over the years, as Julie's condition deteriorated, advocacy work became physically harder. Getting out of the house took its toll. She did as much as she could, but newer patients were more physically able and could take up the charge.

But year after year, the law would get passed in the Senate and stymied in the House. They were about two votes short. She would hear the same objections every year and the same anxieties about what would happen if the bill did pass: "Look at California," people would say to her, referring to the chaos that ensued there as dispensaries got shut down by the feds, since federal law doesn't recognize the state laws.

But according to Julie, the problem with Illinois is that it doesn't have a referendum. The states that have gotten it passed have had a referendum; the people could vote it in. And yet it's a hard issue to get people to rally around.

"How do you get chronically ill people to storm the Capitol about cannabis?" she asks, laughing. "It's not like the teachers' union."

Last December, Julie was falling a lot. She had what she calls a "mini exacerbation," a relapse of some of her symptoms, and had to go into a nursing home and the hospital. She returned home at the end of March.

What Julie knows about California is that in the dispensaries, there is a much greater level of sophistication about which brand of pot treats which ailment. With all those crazy brands—Lemon Skunk, White Diesel, Maui, Alien Dawg, Girl Scout Cookies, White Widow, Purple Urkle, Northern Lights—which in Illinois are hard to grow, it's easier to cure yourself. Plus, people are just throwing leaves away because everyone's focusing on the buds.

She sighs. "Get me to California right now."

Ken Robbins

Philip Spitzer worked from 1966 to 1969 as a literary agent for John Cushman Associates, then the American affiliate of Curtis, Brown, London, representing hundreds of British writers. In 1969 he formed the Philip G. Spitzer Literary Agency, representing a wide range of fiction and nonfiction writers, as well more than a dozen French publishers. He specializes in general fiction and literary crime fiction, as well as the nonfiction subjects of politics, sports, and works of sociological interest. This is his first *written* work of fiction.

tips for the pot-smoking traveler
by philip spitzer

My wife and I rarely travel without weed. In spite of all the risks and possible consequences involved, it's nothing next to traveling without it. After all, my wife and I met in Paris—but we might not have without the weed. Since that worked out positively, why change it?

Our prescription still reads, *Take two a day or as needed.*

Like anyone else, we have had our share of close calls whether alone or together. And this story is about close calls, although the episodes are not intended to be a deterrent.

Last Exit to Brussels
or
Tip #1: Check Your Weed's Potency

In 1984, I was traveling to Paris to visit my family. I had to find the most reasonable fare, which turned out to be round-trip to Brussels and a train from Brussels to Paris. I was only going to be in Paris for a week, and so I brought along one ounce of pot, which I casually slipped into my jacket pocket. While still at JFK airport in New York. I had plenty of time to roll a joint, step outside, and have a smoke. The ounce being a last-minute addition, I wasn't certain of its strength. It turned out to be high-voltage pot, enough to induce paranoia, which I was not used to. During the night flight I imagined that someone of authority had seen me smoke, followed me to the plane with the intention of making an arrest in Brussels, where the consequences would surely be more severe.

Unlike the usual calming effect of the drug, I was unable to sleep, one eye open the entire flight. As I arrived in the Brussels train station, I was still scanning my surroundings to make sure I was not being followed. Like a spy or a fugitive, I made my way across the station, every passerby a possible threat.

My train ticket put me in a compartment with three other travelers, each of whom left at various stops in Belgium, and I soon found myself comfortably alone and finally relaxed.

Just as I was dozing off, there was a knock on the compartment door. It opened up to reveal a police officer standing in the corridor, mumbling something about drugs! Had I really been followed, after all? Had one of my fellow passengers, smelling the weed in my pocket, turned me in? Or was I experiencing the lingering paranoia of the joint I had smoked hours earlier? All of these possibilities (along with the rest of my life behind the bars of a Brussels prison) flashed before my eyes, ending with my bulging, odiferous jacket pocket no more than a meter from the police officer's nose.

It took me awhile to come to my senses and understand that the officer needed to use my compartment to strip-search a passenger suspected of having drugs. I welcomed the officer, but not until I had already fled to the relatively fresh air of the corridor where I managed to stop shaking and consider the irony of my situation

(Rule #4: Never confess until asked.)

Would I even put myself in such a situation again? *But of course!*

Club Med or Bust

or

Tip #2: Talcum Powder Is Best Applied Dried

Like everyone else, my wife and I have discovered all sorts of ways of concealing our pot while traveling, just about everything short of disabling dogs at the airport. But one of our best efforts came close to landing us in a Mexican jail.

It was 1990 and we were traveling to a Club Med in southwestern Mexico. We knew that the nearest village was as tiny as it was remote, and we suspected that the Club Med (especially this one, focused on middle-aged guests and families with children) would not be a likely place to score drugs. My wife had rolled a dozen joints and buried them in a container of talcum powder. Safe enough, it would seem, especially if you considered the profile of the passengers: Screaming children and fat, middle-aged fathers wearing basketball jerseys and sneakers that looked to be size Shaq. A motley middle-class group that the authorities would surely ignore.

Customs was situated outside the terminal building ("terminal," in this case, seeming like the operative word). We disembarked and took our place in a line, which snaked back almost to the plane. The building was hidden from our sight by various types of shrubbery, as if intentionally camouflaged. When the station itself finally came into view, we were shocked to see what was taking place. As each passenger took a turn before the agents, he or she was asked to press a large button of sorts, in plain view of everyone else. If the light that came on green, the passenger could pass through without inspection. If the light was red, the passenger was ushered to the side and his baggage was inspected. But not just inspected. Every item of clothing, every pocket, every gadget or container, was taken apart and pored over. Was a cavity search next? Possibly. Probably.

I broke out in a cold sweat, as did my wife. My trembling hands quickly surveyed the pockets of my jacket and trousers, which I had not worn for some time. Of course, each of the pockets on my jacket harbored at least one roach, which I managed to drop into the bushes as we inched along the path. I kept picturing the agents opening that container of talcum powder, laughing their asses off triumphantly, then checking *our* asses, and finally leading us off to a damp, stony prison cell (without a cell phone, without a call to our embassy, without our lawyer or our families). We would surely spend the rest of our lives there, dreaming of Club Med cocktails on the beach at sunset while we dined on tostada gruel and Montezuma's Revenge water.

My wife and I walked up and hit the dreaded button together, holding our collective breath. I can still see my shaking hand reach for the button, which somehow turned green. A miracle. We could breathe again—though I think it was several minutes before either one of us did.

(Rule #2a: Whether you are traveling to Club Med, Disney World, or even on a Carnival cruise, do not take anything for granted.)

Did I learn my lesson? *Of course not.*

The Safety of Amsterdam
or
Tip #3: Don't Skip the Dry Cleaners

I was going to be in Belgium for a business meeting and asked my wife to join me. After the three-day meeting, we would take a train to Amsterdam for a few days. The business part of the trip was going to be serious and boring; thus, no need to bring along any reefer. (Why waste good weed on boring business meetings?)

Business concluded, we headed to Amsterdam, just a few days into the trip. The train ride was long and tiresome, a local as it turned out that stopped frequently in Belgium and then Holland. We had planned to get to Amsterdam in time to check in to our hotel and then go out to dinner, and though the train ride seemed to take forever we made it in time, the trip uneventful.

The hotel turned out to be old and beautiful and we were told there was a wonderful restaurant just across the canal. As we were unpacking, my wife asked me if I had a light for her cigarette. I didn't, as I hadn't wanted to lose yet another lighter to US Customs.

But as I was going through my valise, I found a match box I didn't remember bringing along, and I handed it to my wife, who opened it and said, "What the hell is this?!"

It turned out to be packed tight with pot. Then, looking in my shoulder bag, I found a rolled joint, along with a roach or two. Of course, we were safe in Amsterdam, a city that has been attracting pot smokers for years. But needless to say, the businesspeople with whom I was meeting in Antwerp would not have looked kindly upon me if I had missed my plane out of JFK or was stopped entering Belgium because of a drug violation. Once again luck was on my side—or in this case, ignorance was bliss.

(Rule #10 or 11 [I've lost count]: Unpack your bags before loading up for another trip!)

But here's a fact, the truth, whatever you want to call it. I am a man of serious aches and pains, an actual condition that has impeded my walking, and pot is my medicine. I swear. I could no more walk the cobblestone streets of Europe than I could walk on air, something the drug makes possible. Should I move to California, or better yet, Washington or Colorado? Maybe. The only problem is getting there. Plane? Train?

And then there was the time I found four kilos of cocaine on a beach in Miami. But that's another story for another time.

Happy traveling!

Julianna Ellman

Thad Ziolkowski is the author of *Our Son the Arson,* a collection of poems, the memoir *On a Wave,* which was a finalist for the PEN/Martha Albrand Award in 2003, and *Wichita,* a novel. In 2008, he was awarded a fellowship from the John S. Guggenheim Memorial Foundation. His essays and reviews have appeared in the *New York Times, Slate, Bookforum, Artforum, Travel & Leisure,* and *Index*. He directs the writing program at Pratt Institute.

jacked
by thad ziolkowski

The rental's GPS declares with satisfaction that I have *reached my destination* but all I can make out, along both sides of the road, is scrub and evergreens. Which might be funny if I weren't so sleep deprived and cranky. With the canceled connecting flight in Salt Lake City, it's taken two days to get here instead of one.

Assuming I'm here. Finally, in the shadow of a spruce (or fir or larch or whatever) I spot the mailbox and cattle gate my brother described. I get out of the car, unhitch the rope keeping the gate closed, walk the gate open, get back in the car, and drive through onto the dirt road on the far side. Then I get out and close the gate, rehitching the rope, and get back in the rental. At which point a phrase from Marx comes to mind: *The idiocy of rural life*.

The dirt road has a strip of mossy grass running up the center and seems cut into forest primeval. Ever since he quit following the Dead around, Justin has lived in outposts like this. We've seen each other three times over the past fifteen years and if I hadn't visited him—once in Alaska, twice in Kauai—we likely wouldn't have seen each other at all. But he's eleven years my junior and I've always felt a parental sort of obligation to meet him more than halfway, to shrug off the unanswered e-mails and unacknowledged gifts. Until recently he's been too broke, working in restaurants, then as an apprentice cabinetmaker, to afford trips to New York. (I'll pass over in silence the bluegrass festival he somehow managed to attend in Kentucky.) But the fact is, I've been only marginally less poor myself all these years, endlessly adjuncting and paying off student loans, and I've gradually gotten fed up with the asymmetry of things between us.

As the car crests a rise, the house appears swathed in fading milky sunlight, a modern two-story, familiar from photos, the wide rolling lawn and guest cottage. Half a dozen pickups and cars are parked in the upward-sloping driveway. A barn in the distance, a greenhouse. Dirt bikes and an ATV in the side yard. I know how recent and precarious this prosperity is, but seeing the spread in person releases a shot of envy mixed with something like shame that prickles my cheeks unpleasantly. The contrast with my monastic room in the group loft on Manhattan's Avenue D is just too stark. I'm possessed by an impulse to back down the driveway and slip away before I'm noticed, somehow call the whole thing off from afar.

But Justin emerges grinning from the two-car garage. He's cut short his long hair and shaved off his beard and looks, in T-shirt and jeans and work boots, younger than thirty-five but more plausibly proprietary. Getting out of the rental to greet him, I smile through my baser emotions and as we embrace they fall away—for the most part. Holding him, feeling the physical reality of his shoulders and back and head, is soothing and bracing in an elemental way I can't seem to retain between visits. Which is the point of visits, especially now: our mother is dead, our brother, Justin's father. We're all that's left of our immediate family.

"Man, sorry about the canceled flight," he says. "What a drag!"

"Not at all—I got to hang in decadent Salt Lake City for the night."

He laughs in the coughing way he has, meanwhile pulling back to search my face. "Hey, wanna check out the garden before it gets dark?"

"Not really."

He stands squinting at me uncertainly.

"Jesus, I'm kidding!" I say. "Of course I want to see your precious garden!"

Justin delivers a half-speed martial arts kick to my rib cage and I'm reminded that if he winds up going to prison he'll be able to defend himself. He leads the way to the acreage behind the house and a pair of Australian sheep dogs I also know from photos falls into step with us—handsome but on the small, mellow side for guard dogs, at least compared to the New York pit bulls I'm used to. Irrigation lines run along ground littered with white plastic buckets, torn bales of hay, shovels, pitchforks.

We come to a kind of signboard affixed with what turns out to be ten or so medical marijuana certificates, each in its own plastic envelope: *Patient, Caregiver, Registry Number, State Seal*. They look like play money. The plants themselves are just beyond, enormous, bushy things wrapped in green plastic skirts, the bud-heavy stalks held aloft by lengths of twine tied to stakes. Beyond the pot, the forest primeval again, where night has already fallen.

It's obvious at a glance that there's more here than these notional ten patients could smoke in a lifetime, which I knew was the deal, but the surplus is so flagrant that my surprise must show.

"It's the backbone of the local economy, so the sheriff's not gonna touch it," Justin says. "And the feds are busting people with forty *thousand* plants, not forty."

I nod as if reassured, but to my big-brother ears this sounds pat, like someone else's words.

"Mold and thieves is what you worry about," Justin says now, as if to add realist heft. I follow along as he makes a quick tour of the patch, pointing out the stumps of ten plants harvested a week ago.

"What *about* those thieves?" I ask. There's no perimeter fence that I can see. In addition to being suddenly colder, it's also gotten spooky out here, evergreens in thrusting, spiky silhouette against the midnight-blue sky, psychedelic foliage whispering in a rising breeze. Relatively small or not, this patch must be worth over a million. Past my mind's eye flickers an image of Mexican cartel soldiers slipping balaclavas over their heads.

"Yeah, well, motherfuckers *love to jack* right about now, when you've done all the backbreaking work and it's ready to harvest." He lifts his chin at a pup tent I hadn't noticed. "That's why I post somebody out here every night."

"Armed?"

"Just with a cell phone. I don't allow guns on the property."

"That's a relief." Or is it? How does he impose his no-guns rule on gunslingers?

The highest buds are so tall that he has to stand on tiptoe to reach their drooping, bristling tips. If I were a pothead, I'd be salivating, but I have if anything an aversion to the cannabis high, which tends to maroon me in my own head. Tenderly thumbing back leaves, Justin peers at a bud through a kind of jeweler's loop.

"The sugary hairs are made up of what they call tricomes—a bit like shrooms. Here." He has me take a peek but all I can see in the dim light is something like blurred rice vermicelli.

"You want all your trikes to be cloudy; none clear," he explains, as if partly to himself, peering through the loop again. "With the right ratio, amber mixed in with cloudy. Leaving them up for a single day can make a subtle but big difference."

He steps back and surveys the plot. "These are coming down tomorrow." His tone is so momentous I nearly let out a laugh. But I've never rolled the dice on anything of this magnitude. If the quality of the pot and therefore his reputation ride on this decision, I guess he has every right to be solemn.

And with that we turn back toward the house, all of whose

windows are now cozily lit. Trotting ahead, the dogs seem as relieved as I am to be leaving the ominous outdoors behind.

The living room is cluttered with sleeping bags and knapsacks. The scent of high-grade weed hangs like incense in the air but vaporizers are the new bong and the air isn't smoky. The crew of trimmers, ranging from teenaged to grizzled, sits at a long wood table in the center of which is a pile of dried pot. Placing a hand on my shoulder, Justin says, "Hey everybody, this is my brother Darius, all the way from New York!"

"The Big Apple!" a guy calls out as if it's a password, though it's something only tourists ever say—some crass, Tammany Hall–era image of plenitude and opportunity, "action."

There's the usual slightly puzzled smiles as they look from me to Justin and back. We have different fathers and bear little obvious resemblance to each other. They call out greetings and wave, then Justin points to each one and tells me his or her name—Jai, Toph, etc.—which I'm too tired to bother trying to keep straight.

Justin's new girlfriend is tending a cauldron of ratatouille in the kitchen. I know her name is Serena and she makes jewelry but I've yet to see a photo of her. It turns out that she looks enough like our mother at thirty that I stand frowning as she delightedly sets aside a wooden spoon and comes forward to give me a long, tight hug.

"I'm so glad you're here," she whispers in my ear. "Justin really needs you right now."

A bit annoyed at her presumption, I pull back and smile insipidly into her soulful gaze until, with what seems like a sigh of slight disappointment, she releases me to Justin, who shows me to a bedroom down the hall, where his two kids by a former girlfriend must stay on their visits, given the bunk bed and stuffed animals and Nerf guns.

He asks whether I want to crash for a bit and I answer by flopping backward onto the lower bunk. I'm expecting to plummet into sleep but once my eyes are shut I start counting money: Justin's paying me twenty-five dollars an hour to trim. I have no idea how much I can do, but I'm hoping to clear a grand, which will put a small dent in my credit card and student loan debt. But with the canceled flight, my earning time has been reduced from five days to four.

I find a bathroom down the hall, take an overdue piss, splash cold water on my face, and go back to the trimming station, where Justin, giving guard-duty instructions to a young, rather stoned-looking guy, points out a pot of coffee and a free chair next to Dolly, a middle-aged woman wearing a tricorn pirate's hat. The scene is more festive now, with beers being cracked open and the carbs of vaporizors loaded with one or another strain of Justin's weed.

Billy, a young guy Justin met in Kauai and seems to have made his factotum, waxes on to no one in particular about how grateful he is to have been brought into the business, being able to help all the "patients" who need their "medicine"; it sure beats working in restaurants, though of course everything can get boring if you do it enough times, even giving massages to the cheerleading squad. At which point Justin sends him out to guard the garden for the night and I'm spared any more of the kid's soft-porn philosophizing.

I watch Dolly's chubby hands, the left holding a bud of kush and rotating it while the right snips rapidly away at the stems using short-sheered scissors with orange finger-grips. "You basically give 'em a haircut." She holds the trimmed bud up for my inspection. "He's in the army now!"

"So he's going *back* to Afghanistan," I say.

"Ha-ha!" she laughs after a beat. "Your brother's funny!" she calls to Justin.

"So you're a professor?" Josh or maybe Jai asks me from across the table.

"Sort of," I say, starting in on a bud with my own pair of scissors. "I'm an adjunct professor."

"What's that?"

"A part-time fool," I say with no more than the usual bitterness, but in this mild, agrarian company it sounds jarringly harsh. They stare at me blinkingly. Well, let them run around the city between two or three colleges for a decade, too worn down to publish and with no hope now of getting a tenure-track job. The only reason I'm "free" to be here is that one of my classes was canceled at the last second.

"Better than a full-time fool!" says a Deadhead Methuselah in a knit rasta cap. He barks out a laugh as if he's startled himself with his own wit, then repeats the remark a few times lest anyone fail to savor it.

For a while I work well enough on coffee and cinnamon toast, and when that no longer stokes my brain fires I begin sniffing around for something stronger. Every month on payday I treat myself to a mingy half-gram from my dealer Richard or one of the local coke bodegas if Richard doesn't pick up and I have a nose for who's holding. As it turns out, no one is, but the verging-on-gaunt girl in the corner has a prescription bottle full of Adderall. She waves away my offer to pay for half a dozen and I'm soon buzzing along more or less oblivious to the tedium.

As people begin dragging themselves off to sleep, Justin pulls up a chair and trims alongside me. How he stays up I'm not sure—sheer drive to see the harvest through, from what I can tell. Dropping the finished buds into a Rubbermaid tub labeled *Willie's Wonder,* we chat about this and that until he broaches the inevitable subject of our mother, who died of a staph infection in Hawaii three years ago, just when Justin was getting his pot plantation underway.

"I just wish she could've been here for a harvest," he says quietly, though the other trimmers are listening to music on earbuds and can't hear us.

"She'd be so proud of you, man," I say.

Justin lets his head fall forward and his shoulders heave.

"She would have cooked for everyone round the clock," I say, rubbing his back with resin-sticky hands, "and trimmed until she got carpal tunnel."

Pinching the bridge of his nose, he nods. "I know."

"And she probably would've wanted to be one of the runners too."

"She would have, wouldn't she?" he says, brightening.

"Which would've been brilliant, because who'd suspect a seventy-year-old lady?"

"Or a professor," he adds with a wink.

"Yeah, right."

We lapse into silence, each missing her in our own way, or perhaps in exactly the same way, who knows? Then Justin heads off to his room with Serena in tow and I'm left in the company of a few fellow speed-eaters.

As dawn breaks outside, Serena reappears bearing a large wooden jewelry display box. She's making everyone gifts to commemorate the harvest. She has a few of the sort of silver heavy-metal rings I've secretly liked but have never even tried on, and I pick out a molten-looking one.

"Your hands are shaking," she says, slipping the ring on my finger. She goes into kitchen and comes back with a mug of what looks and smells like herbal tea but almost certainly has some cannabis infusion mixed into it. I'm too whacked to care. "This will steady you up." And it does.

Then in comes Billy-from-Kauai. He looks shaken but I don't know him well enough to be sure.

"Billy, what's up?" Serena asks.

He has trouble catching a breath. "Where's Justin?" he says finally.

"Justin's in bed. What's *up*?"

"We got jacked!"

"Jacked? Where were you?"

"I was asleep!"

"Oh, Billy!"

"Where's Justin, man?"

Serena rushes into the back of the house, followed by Billy, and they reemerge seconds later led by Justin, who runs out the back door with a pistol in his hand.

"Justin!" I shout, but if he hears me he doesn't show any sign of it and is rumbling down the stairs to the ground floor. After a stoned pause to gather my wits, I go after them but make a wrong turn and wind up on the driveway in front of the house, and when I run around to the back and the garden, Justin and the other two have had a quick look at the scene of the crime and driven off with a snarl I can hear from where I stand looking at the stumps of the thirty plants. I call him on my cell phone but he's not picking up.

Dolly and the Deadhead Methuselah join me. "Oh my God!" wails Dolly, and her tricorn slips off her head.

Methuselah covers his eyes with both hands. "Holy shit!" But there's an undercurrent of excitement in their reaction too, the schadenfreude of hired hands.

"Well, he told us they were coming down today . . ." Dolly says, shaking her head.

"He just didn't say who was cutting 'em down," Methuselah finishes for her. Crouching bandy-leggedly, he points to sweeping marks in the dirt. "Look, they drug 'em off this way!"

We follow the trails to the edge of the woods, which have an innocent state-park character in the morning light.

Methuselah says, "I told him: put up a fence or leave the dogs tied up out here. Or both!"

"Didn't want to listen," Dolly says. At which point the dogs saunter up. "Where the fuck were you?" The dogs wag their tails happily at the acknowledgment.

"Folks live in these woods," Methuselah explains, squinting into piney shadows crosscut with dim bars of sunlight.

"Sort of half-hippie, half-*Deliverance*," Dolly adds.

A bit like you two, I think.

When Justin, Billy, and Serena get home it's late afternoon. Most of the trimmers have left. Justin dismisses the rest, including Dolly and Methuselah, who have been doing more smoking and jabbering than working anyway.

"Okay," Justin tells us in the kitchen. "We need to go to Plan B now."

"Which is what?" I ask. Serena and Billy look just as clueless. "And where's the gun?"

Justin lifts the hem of his T-shirt: it's tucked into the waistband of his jeans.

"Give it to me," I say, and to my surprise he hands it over. I just want to get it away from him but I find I like the feel of it. Engraved on the barrel in stylized letters: *Glock*.

"Plan B," Justin says, "is we sell the trimmed weed to folks we have in Denver and Detroit, pay off people we owe, and do a quick indoor grow to recoup the loss from the jacking. And I want Billy to make the run."

Even Billy the fuck-up looks stunned.

"Billy deserves a chance to redeem himself," Justin says.

Serena is staring pleadingly at me but there's no need.

Two days later I'm driving into Denver with ten pounds in the trunk, triple-bagged, vacuum-sealed, wrapped in newspaper, and buried under sacks of organic fruit. After Denver, Detroit; and after Detroit, New York, the Big Apple.